How to Recognize a Demon Has Become Your Friend

Originally published by

NECON
ebooks
www.neconebooks.com

How to Recognize a Demon Has Become Your Friend

by Linda Addison

Cover & Interior Art
by Jill Bauman

ALWAYS A GIFT

Little
Free
Library®

NEVER FOR SALE

Necon Modern Horror #9

Originally Published by Necon E-Books
This Edition Published by Six Star Tree Publications

*This collection is dedicated to Bob Booth, the Necon Gang
and all my friends and family who have wrapped me in love…*

Copyright Acknowledgments

Table of Contents

Introduction

I've always loved words. When I was in school and the teacher gave me a copy of my first book, "See Dick Run" kind of book. I remember holding it and knowing I wanted to make things like this without understanding what that meant. I did know it told a story and my mother was a wonderful storyteller who would make up tales, and include us children as characters.

I still love words. I've been known to take the titles of friends' books and turn them into a poem. Some find it amusing and/or perplexing. I just like playing with words.

From Linda to Linda

One Night at Sheri-Too-Long's Popcorn Bar
    after Working Up the Corporate Ladder
I ordered a Pullus Cogens on the rocks,
    having failed to Recognize my Friend had Become a Demon
I became a Ghost Driving Sharp, Shiny Hurting Things
    down a endless road of 369 Gates of Hell.

In this Night of the Living and Dead
    I was Just Passing Through, Unrequited and sad,
what little Power was left in me was more of a Mourning Meal,
    sprinkled with ground Land Sharks, the band 'Milez To Go'
played, Little Red from the Hood danced with Comic Cannibals,
    Am I Repeating Myself?

There is no Future or Past, just me and The Forever Dead
    wishing we had bottled Up De Evil,
In This Strange Place, Imperfect and weak, I want to
    Live and Let Live, but Demons Dance with Animated Objects,
Bending into the Fire/Fight around me, I wish I had recognized
    a Demon had Become my Friend, so I could return,
Dust to Dust, to Galaxy A.G.2 and the peace of mortality.

— *Linda Addison*

Linda Addison

How to Recognize a Demon
Has Become Your Friend

Song from their open mouth makes you sleep,
upon waking you feel empty and sad,
    there is a mark of ash on your chest
    where your heart should be.

Their eyes remind you of hunger,
but everything you eat has no taste,
    your eyes reflect flames in the mirror
    you stare at the sun, but it doesn't hurt.

They ask you for the time
but you tell them when you were born,
    suddenly you can't remember
    your mother or father.

Your other friends stop calling you,
their faces flash as 'Missing' online,
    you change your status to
    'Possessed' on your social network.

When you walk past a church with them
you feel sick and have to cross the street,
    they joke about being allergic to old
    buildings, you laugh with them.

One day you blink and you have no breath,
memories of your life fade like a dream,
    all you see is red sky, ash under your feet
    and in their burning arms you cannot cry.

Dust to Dust

My remains have been rudely thrust into the ground without a coffin. There is something unfinished about the whole thing. I wish I could remember dying.

Gasses created in my intestines churn through useless blood vessels and dead tissue, inflating what was a thin body into something large and misshapen. My body fluids leak from every opening into the surrounding earth. There is life in me still, if I count the maggots feasting inside. I must smell and look horrible.

I now know where the soul lives. The enduring bones. Through my bones I'm connected to the earth around me. I hear the murmuring of others, their bones talking, praying, and calling out. The earth answers us, singing warmth and security.

Distant voices of pain cry in deep sadness. There is some horror there, I fear. Are they in Hell? It's hard to imagine the earth that has been my comfort giving pain. The screams of those tortured souls recedes.

I measure time by the changes in the soft mass surrounding my bones. Gas-filled organs rupture and leak from under skin slippery with large blisters. Escaping fluid purges my maggot guests and allows the earth to move closer. I can't wait until these soft parts rot away, to have all of my bones touched by earth. Here and there my skeleton is exposed.

Grains of dirt caress parts of my skull and fingers free of skin and tissue. The joy and peace flowing to me is like no feeling I can remember before I died.

There is randomness to my memory of the other side. The memories are fleeting, filled with the needs of the breathing soft body that covered my bones when I was alive. Moments of happiness and pain entangle, making the memories all but meaningless to capture. Nothing like the tranquility the earth gives me. The song of earth's souls surrounding me is more beautiful than anything I've ever experienced. I could spend eternity with this song.

All the rotting meat is gone. Finally my bones are touched by earth. I am complete. The only thing better will be when my bones crumble and mix with the earth.

There is a subtle change in the song around me. It's becoming distant. A white light covers my bones. The light comes towards me. There are others in the light.

Linda Addison

I'm being pulled into the light, back to the other side. I'm losing all of this. I don't want to be smothered in organs, muscles and skin again. I don't want to become deaf to the songs, to be a single, lonely body again.

I start to cry...

Mourning Meal

She was so hungry
    raw nothingness
growing at her center.

Eating began with simple things
    a kindergarten drawing
the yellow construction paper crunchy.

The plastic badge from swimming class
    chewy at first
its silver foil edge caught in her teeth.

The handmade Mother's Day card
    smelled sweet
its crayon words tasted bitter.

One toy spaceman
    bitten into little pieces
swallowed like strange pills.

She ate her way through his trail
    piece by sheet
but still the hunger scratched inside.

Each memory lingered
    like the sweet herbs she used
in his favorite meal.

Soup she would never make again
    like his face
she would never see again.

The Power

The first time Brenda saw her cousin, Angelique, she looked like a black angel. Dark as sweet chocolate, dressed in shades of cinnamon chiffon. As Angelique stood at the top of the Amtrak train stairs, Brenda took one look at her and knew she had the Power. It glimmered around her. She glanced at her father. He obviously didn't see how special Angelique was; even Angelique seemed unaware of the strength of the sparkling light she threw out that Saturday morning.

"Angelique, is that you?" Brenda's father lifted the girl from the train to the ground. The layers of her dress floated in the air like wings. "Look how you've grown. Last time I saw you, you were only as tall as a dream, and now you and your cousin Brenda are growing like rainbows into the sky."

Brenda was used to her father talking like poetry, every now and then. Grandmom said he was one of those people who'd been born in a moment of luminosity and had no choice. He was an artist who made things out of anything he found on the street, and taught elementary school. Fortunately, Brenda was never in his classes, but Grandmom said that was just the way it should be, plain and simple, and Brenda should thank her mother in heaven for looking after her.

A porter carried Angelique's suitcases to the platform.

"Girl, your mother sent you with enough clothes for a year, and you're only here for the summer. That's just like Julia." He laughed. "This is a beautiful dress, but I hope you got some playing-around clothes."

"Yes, sir," Angelique said.

"In North Carolina that's the polite thing to say, but there are no 'sirs' here in Philly. Uncle Larry will do. Okay?"

"Yes, Uncle Larry," she said slowly.

"How are your Mom and Dad?" he asked.

"Mother is busy with her charity work, and Father's business is doing very well." Angelique smoothed her dress.

"Good. Now let's get you home so your grandmother can take a look at you. She's cooked quite a feast in your honor."

Larry picked up as many suitcases as he could carry; the porter trailed behind with the rest.

Brenda took Angelique's hand and pulled her along with them. "I'm so happy you're here. You're staying in my room. I've got two beds. We can be like twin sisters, just like our moms really were."

"I'd like that." Angelique squeezed Brenda's hand.

When they reached the parking lot Larry paid the porter and packed the suitcases in the car. Angelique whispered in Brenda's ear, "Do you know that old woman following us?"

"Where?" Brenda asked.

"Behind me, across the street." Angelique turned around. "She's gone now, but she was staring at us on the train platform."

"I didn't notice her." Brenda shrugged. "Could've been anybody."

As they drove to West Philadelphia, Brenda talked about all the fun they would have over the summer. They pulled into a driveway next to a three floor wood house off Lancaster Avenue. As they stepped out of the car, their grandmother waved to them from the porch.

She gathered Angelique into her strong arms and gave her a huge hug. Her deep laugh echoed on the porch as she held Angelique at arm's length.

"Girl, look at you. Grown up enough at twelve to travel by yourself." She shook her head while smiling.

Larry carried some suitcases to the porch and went back to the car for the rest.

"Everyone grab a bag," Grandmom said.

The house was filled with the smell of roasted chicken and apple pie. Grandmom settled in the green velvet couch and made Angelique sit next to her. "Now, let's give your mother a call."

"I'll do it." Angelique picked up the phone.

"Hello, Mother.

"Yes, the train ride was fine.

"No, I won't forget.

"Yes, Mother." Angelique said several times as she chewed the corner of her right thumb.

"Goodbye." She handed the phone to her grandmother.

"Hi, honey.

"Oh, you worry too much. Nobody is running wild here. Her and Brenda will have a great summer." She winked at Angelique.

"We'll give you a call next week. Bye sweetie."

She patted Angelique's hand. "That daughter of mine always did worry too much. You know I think it'll be good for both of you to have a little space. Now let's eat some of this food I've been cooking."

The dining room table was set up with the good china and silverware on a white lace tablecloth. White candles stood in crystal candle holders and a crystal bowl filled with daisies decorated the center of the table.

"It looks like Thanksgiving," Angelique said.

"And that's just what it is, child, because we're thankful to have you here." She hugged Angelique. "You girls wash your hands and help me bring out the vegetables."

The doorbell rang. Larry answered it and the house filled with the sounds of children and adults as his two brothers and their families came in.

The evening went like a family reunion, everyone talking and eating. Angelique answered everyone's questions politely, smiled shyly and stayed near Brenda or her grandmother. After dessert, the adults sat in the living room drinking and smoking while the children played checkers in the dining room.

Everyone left around nine and their grandmother sent the girls to bed, saying Angelique was tired from all that traveling and Brenda from being so excited.

The next morning, after breakfast, Brenda asked, "Can we go to the video store, Grandmom? I want to show Angelique around the neighborhood. "

"That's fine, just be back home by lunch time."

"We will," Brenda said.

They walked to the corner of the block. They passed a couple of neighbors working in their yard, but once they turned onto Lancaster Avenue the sidewalk was full of people. Brenda and Angelique looked in the windows of the shoe and clothes store, and ran into some of Brenda's friends on the way to the video rental store. They spent a long time looking at the new movie and game releases before picking an action movie to rent.

On the way home they heard a shuffling behind them. Brenda looked backwards quickly. "It's that crazy old lady from across the street."

Angelique glanced at the woman. "That's the woman I saw at the train station."

Brenda frowned. "Just ignore her." She pointed at a small deli on the corner. "Let's get some sodas."

When they came out of the store, the woman was not in sight. They turned the next corner onto the block of their house. The old woman limped out from behind a large oak tree. She was dressed in layers, torn red pants under a gray dress and dirty beige sweater.

She gestured with a bent finger at them. "You shoulda been my sweet girl. I be teaching you right stuff—make good use of all that sweet sparkly breathing out of your skin. She won't show you all the light - dark makings." She spat in the direction of their house.

"Mrs. Johnston, we need to get home," Brenda said, pulling Angelique around the woman.

"Don't you worry, it ain't you I got the problem with. Keep up your learning. Yeah, that's what you do, my shiny diamonds. I follow your light. You my pretty key." She laughed through a mouth of missing teeth.

They heard her shrill laughter as they rushed down the street. When they turned around she was gone. They sat on the porch to get their breath.

"What was she talking about?" Angelique asked.

"Don't pay any attention to her. She's been strange every since I can remember. People say she lost her mind when her husband and son died in a car accident." Brenda pointed to a broken down house across the street. "That's her place."

The yard was overgrown with weeds and a wild rose bush covering the front porch. A couple of windows were broken and paint peeled from the wood frame.

"That house doesn't look like anyone lives in it," Angelique said. "Are you sure she's not dangerous?"

"She can't hurt us, we're protected."

"What do you mean?"

"I'll explain later, let's get lunch." Brenda unlocked the front door.

After lunch, Brenda asked, "Grandmom, can we go to the attic?"

"Okay, honey. Be careful up there." She spread fresh herbs from the garden on the kitchen table.

"We will," Brenda said.

They went up to the second floor. Brenda pulled the attic cord, lowered the stair ladder and scampered up into the dark opening. Angelique took one step and stood at the bottom.

"It's kind of dark," she said.

"Just a minute." Brenda disappeared into the attic and a light came on. After a few seconds she popped her head out of the opening. Angelique was still on the first step. "You coming? There's lots of cool stuff up here."

Angelique stepped up and tottered forward to hold onto the upper steps. "I-I —"

"You've never been on a ladder before?" Brenda asked.

"Ladies don't climb ladders." She held onto the step.

"I don't know about that, but if you want to get to the attic you're going to have to climb this ladder. Here, back off." Brenda climbed back down. "You go up first. Take one step at a time, hold on to the step above if you need, but don't look up or down, just go for the next step until you're at the top. I'll be right behind you. I won't let you fall. I promise."

"Okay." Angelique took each step like a baby learning to climb stairs for the first time, but finally got to the top and pulled herself into the attic.

Boxes, trunks and old furniture crowded the floor. It smelled musty and a fine layer of dust had settled on all the surfaces.

"It's not very clean up here." Angelique touched a carton. She wiped her fingers on her jeans.

"Don't say that too loud. Grandmom will have us up here with a bucket and rags, cleaning." Brenda took a couple of old towels from a box in the corner, threw one at Angelique and used the other to wipe off the top of a wood box. "Some of these things are from when Grandmom moved here to help take care of me after Mommy died."

"Let's see what's in here." She read the label. "'Brenda baby toys', not very interesting. What's that trunk near you say, Angelique?"

She wiped off the dust. "It's my mother's toys."

"Now that's more like it." Brenda unbuckled the leather straps and flipped open the trunk. The acrid scent of mothballs drifted into the air.

There were baby blankets on top, inside plastic bags. Underneath were baby clothes in shades of pink, yellow and white. They stacked them on the floor. At the bottom they found a rag doll and other toys. The material of its body was made from worn blue flannel, with brown yarn hair, button eyes, red felt lips and faded red flannel dress.

"I've never imagined my mother playing with dolls," Angelique said.

"Well, Aunt Julia definitely played with this doll." Brenda handed the doll to Angelique. "There's more toys in here." She pulled out stuffed animals, a wooden pull car with a frayed cord, a metal tobacco tin filled with marbles and ribbons.

Angelique touched each toy but kept the doll in her lap. She carried the doll tucked under her arm as they investigated other boxes, finding old clothes and dish sets. Brenda went through the drawers of a dresser and discovered a small red bag tied with white cord. She brought it to the light and sniffed it.

"What's that?" Angelique asked, putting her mother's doll on an old trunk.

Brenda carefully untied the bag and emptied its contents in a teacup. It was a ball of white wax with little bits of what looked like sticks lodged in it.

"It's a conjure ball. Looks like a spell of protection."

"How do you know that?" Angelique said.

"Don't you know the power runs strong in our family? That's what Grandmom says."

"Magic isn't real."

"It's real enough. Grandmom says I'm too young, but I've learned a lot about magic online." She dropped the ball back into the bag and tied it close. "Can't you feel the light around this charm? It's been up here for years and it's still glowing." Brenda held the bag up by its cord.

"I don't see anything but an old bag," Angelique said. "Mother says voodoo is uneducated superstition."

"Voodoo isn't the same thing. Anyway, magic is just people using their power, mostly to help others," Brenda said. She took Angelique's hands in hers. "It's inside everybody and everything; some people have it stronger than others. Can't you feel it?"

Brenda put Angelique's hands on her chest and closed her eyes. She took a slow breath. White light flickered behind her closed eyes. Tingling began below her belly button and pulled up through her chest, gathered in her next breath. She pushed out and opened her eyes.

Angelique stood with her eyes closed, smiling. Brenda could feel her light mix with Angelique's and drift into the air around them.

"You see," Brenda said.

Angelique opened her eyes and took a deep breath. "What was that?"

"Me reaching out to you. What did it feel like?"

"Like electricity and light and warmth, like a dream." Angelique held her hands up, looked at each finger.

Brenda saw the warm glow of gold light outline Angelique's hands and it was clear that Angelique finally saw it also.

"This is no more of a dream than any of us see when awake. Grandmom says God is dreaming us all the time."

"That was just a trick." Angelique stepped backwards away from Brenda.

"You know that's not true. You can feel it inside, whether you believe it or not."

"Well, I did feel something. And that glowing..." Angelique sat down on a trunk. "Even if I have this power — what good is it?"

"What do you wish for more than anything?" Brenda asked.

Angelique picked up her mother's rag doll and held her close to her face. She closed her eyes. "I wish–I wish my mother would love me."

"We could do that, Angelique. You and I together could do it."

"You think so. Really?"

Brenda nodded. "She's your mother so she already loves you. It's just locked away inside of her. We can make a gris-gris to open her to you."

"Even though we're here and she's in North Carolina?"

"Distance don't mean a thing. We'll need something that's been close to her."

They both looked at the doll.

"And I have a handkerchief of hers in my suitcase," Angelique said, hugging her mother's doll.

Brenda rubbed the sliver key on the chain around her neck. "Good, then we'll make the charm tonight. I think some of my mother's toys are over there. Let's check it out."

Brenda put the conjure ball back in the dresser. They spent the next two hours going though the trunks, trying on clothes, and setting up old dishes and glasses for pretend meals, until their grandmother called them for dinner.

That night they sat on the back porch eating ice cream while Brenda's father had some friends over after dinner. Jazz played in the background as the adults talked and laughed in the living room. The lightning bugs drifted above the grass and herb garden like stars while the girls ate their ice cream. Crickets sang from the bushes along the back of the yard.

"Make a wish on the next lightning bug and it'll come true," Brenda said.

"Is that more magic?" Angelique asked.

"Naw, just a saying, but it couldn't hurt."

They both whispered wishes and laughed.

Brenda stood up from the wicker chair and peeked into the kitchen window. No one was there.

"Want to make that gris-gris for your mother now?" she asked Angelique.

"Tonight?"

"Why not? It's as good a time as any."

"What if something goes wrong?" Angelique asked.

"First lesson in using the power: your intent makes the magic. It's not a complicated spell anyway."

"I don't know about this—"

"Of course you don't. That's why I'm going to teach you. Come on."

They entered the empty kitchen through the back door. Brenda found a small brown paper bag in the cabinet and sprinkled sugar in it.

"We'll put it together in our bedroom," she whispered.

They walked quickly through the dining room. Larry and his friends were in the living room, laughing and talking over the music. The girls dashed up the stairs. They tiptoed past their grandmother's room, where they could hear her talking on the phone.

In the bedroom, Brenda put a bracelet with little bells on the doorknob. "So we can hear if someone opens the door," she said.

She put the desk lamp on the floor and used the two bedposts to make a tent out of a sheet. They crouched under the sheet.

"Spread the handkerchief on the floor," Brenda said.

Angelique laid the delicate square on the floor. It was white with white lace roses along the edge and her mother's initials sewn in yellow on a corner.

Brenda pulled a light wood box from under the bed; it had a sun painted on it. She took the silver chain with a heart and key from around her neck and unlocked the box.

"I thought that was just a charm necklace," Angelique said.

Brenda winked at her and opened the box. It was filled with yarn, bits of material and things that jangled at the bottom. Brenda took out a ball of red yarn, pulled about twelve inches off, and cut it with a small pair of scissors from the box. She took a little pad of paper and pen out of the box and handed it to Angelique.

"Write your mother's first name nine times, real small."

Angelique wrote her mother's name, in careful strokes.

20

"Now fold the paper up as tight as you can and put it in the middle of the handkerchief," Brenda said. She held the paper bag open. "Take a little sugar and sprinkle it in the handkerchief, to sweeten her to you."

"You have the doll?" Brenda asked.

"Yes." Angelique got the doll from her dresser drawer.

Brenda handed her the scissors. "Cut a tiny piece of the dress and put it in the handkerchief."

Angelique looked at the scissors and the doll.

"Come on, Angelique. Think of it as an experiment, we just need a little bit."

"Okay," she said slowly. She cut a teeny piece of material from the inside hem of the doll's dress and put the threads into the handkerchief. "Just as long as we don't have to sacrifice an animal or cut ourselves for this."

Brenda laughed. "You don't know anything, do you? You don't use blood for a love spell. Fold the handkerchief up."

"Now wrap this yarn around it nine times and put nine knots in it – to hold it forever."

When she was done, Angelique stared at the small package they made.

"You've made your first gris-gris." Brenda tapped it. "The last step is to sleep with it under your mattress."

Angelique slid it under the mattress. "Will it work?"

"Of course, between your power and a perfect gris-gris, it'll work."

Angelique laid the doll on her bed. "How long will it take?"

"You can't put a time on something like this."

The doorknob jangled and they both jumped.

"Brenda?" Her father knocked on the door.

They took a deep breath in relief. Brenda locked the box and slid it back under her bed. "Come in."

"What's this, camping out?" he asked.

"No, Daddy, just swapping secrets."

He smiled, a little too wide, as he leaned against the door. "That's good." He turned to leave and swung in a circle. "Oh, your grandmother wants you two to help her in the kitchen."

"Okay." Brenda put the lamp back on the night stand.

Larry turned and walked away.

Brenda made a sign like drinking with her hand. They both giggled.

"He's funny when he drinks. It doesn't take much. That's why he doesn't drink the hard stuff. Does your dad drink?" Brenda asked.

Angelique nodded. "He likes scotch and soda, two ice cubes. I make it for him when he comes home from work."

"Really? You ever tasted it?"

She made a face. "Yes. I like white wine better. That's what my mother drinks."

"Your mom lets you drink?"

"She gives me a little wine on special occasions, so I can develop my tastes."

Brenda threw the sheet back on the bed. "I've tasted beer. It's all right but I like cherry soda better."

On their way down the stairs, Angelique said, "Shouldn't we check with Grandmom about what we just did?"

"No," Brenda said quickly. "We don't want to bother her about something this small. Okay?"

"Grandmom doesn't know you're doing magic, does she?" Angelique asked slowly.

"Shhhh–do you want it to work or not?"

Angelique nodded.

"Then let's go."

They helped clear the table and wash the dishes. Most of the time one of Larry's friends sat in the kitchen talking to their grandmother about problems with her husband. After they finished drying the dishes, the girls went to bed.

In the bedroom, with the lights out, Angelique asked, "Is it going to work?"

"Don't have any doubt. It's important to be confident."

"Okay. Goodnight."

The rest of the week Angelique tried not to ask Brenda about the gris-gris for her mother. Every night she checked under her mattress to make sure the little white bundle, wrapped in red yarn was still there. They played video games during the day and met with Brenda's friends to jump rope and window shop. At night Brenda showed Angelique her favorite computer sites on spells.

Friday evening the phone rang. Their grandmother called Angelique from the yard.

"It's for you," she said, handing the phone to Angelique.

"Hello, Mother." She told her about the fun things they did, leaving out the magic discussions. Her mother sounded about the same. Angelique gave up all hope.

"Talk to you next week," she said, ready to hang up.

"What?

"Oh. I love you too." She stared at the phone after her mother hung up.

"She said she loves me," she said, hugging her grandmother.

"Well, of course she loves you, honey."

"But, she's never said it before. Never." She ran out of the room to the yard, grabbed Brenda and swung her around. "She loves me. She said she loves me."

They danced in a circle until they collapsed on the grass, out of breath.

"It worked, Brenda, it worked," said Angelique.

"Of course it did. I had no doubt."

The first half of the summer went fast. Between playing, Brenda taught Angelique what she knew about magic. They found spells online for making someone leave, to cure different kinds of sickness. They made a list of the kinds of objects carried in a nation sack. As they played and shopped, they collected unusual rocks from the park or feathers. Every now and then, they would find some interesting piece of metal or glass on the ground and added it to their box of magical material.

They gathered ingredients for small spells, but never put the whole spell together. They saw Mrs. Johnston every couple of weeks; she stared at them from across the street and whispered to herself, but she didn't talk to them again.

Angelique never saw their grandmother doing magic, but every now and then someone came by the house and Grandmom gave them a package wrapped in brown paper. She once saw her grandmother take a small pale blue bag out of her blouse, rub it and put it back. Brenda said that her was her nation sack, where she carried special things for protection.

Every time Angelique's mother called she told her she loved her, and even said she missed her.

One hot July day, Brenda and Angelique came in the house laughing, after a day at the park, and found their grandmother in the hallway on the floor. Her chest was covered with a dark cloud of squirming snakes. The girls screamed and the snakes melted away.

Brenda ran to her grandmother's unconscious body and shook her, yelling, "Grandmom!"

Angelique ran to the living room and called '911'. The ambulance came quickly. Grandmom's friend from next door rushed in when the medics arrived. She called Larry's school and left a message. Brenda stayed by her grandmother's side as they carried her into the ambulance.

"I need to go with Brenda," Angelique said.

"Go ahead," the neighbor said. "I'll watch the house. Larry will be there as soon as he can. I'll be praying here."

Angelique glanced across the street before getting in the ambulance and saw Mrs. Johnston standing in the shade of a tree, pointing and smiling. When she looked out the back window of the ambulance the old woman was gone. Nausea gripped her stomach. Could that woman have had something to do with this?

The medics had an oxygen mask on their grandmother, but she was still unconscious. Brenda crouched on the floor, held her grandmother's hand, and cried softly. Angelique tried to talk to Brenda, but she pulled away.

At the hospital the doctor made them stay in the waiting room. Brenda held Angelique's hand but still wouldn't talk. The waiting room was filled with men, women and children clutched in little groups. Most stared at magazines or the droning television hanging from the ceiling. The sound of wheels rolling through the corridor broke through the whispers of people comforting each other.

Angelique stared at the door, waiting for someone, anyone, to come in and tell them how their grandmother was doing. Brenda stared at the floor.

Larry walked in, out of breath, as if he had run to the hospital.

"Are you girls alright?" He hugged them both.

"Is Grandmom going to die?" Brenda whispered.

"No, your grandmother is the strongest person on this planet. I have to talk to her doctor. I wanted to make sure you two were okay first."

"We'll be fine, Uncle Larry," Angelique said.

"I'll be back as soon as I can." He dropped his backpack and rushed out of the room.

Brenda wrapped her arms around herself and started rocking back and forth. "She's going to die. I can feel her – slipping away."

Angelique could also feel the wrongness, like air being sucked out of the room. "Somebody is doing something bad to her. You saw those snakes back at the house, right?"

Brenda nodded her eyes puffy and red from crying.

"Somebody, I think the old woman from across the street, did bad magic against Grandmom. I saw Mrs. Johnston when the ambulance drove away. She was smiling."

"But-but Grandmom's protection should have kept her safe," Brenda whispered.

"I know, but somehow it didn't. Those snakes weren't real, but we saw them. Do you remember reading that sometimes you can see spells working through animal spirits?"

Brenda nodded.

"We can do something about this. We have to do a spell to stop it."

"Maybe," Brenda said. "Maybe we can."

"We'll pray now and later we'll do more." Angelique put her arm around Brenda and closed her eyes.

Someone tapped Angelique on her shoulder.

"Uncle Larry, how is she?"

"They think she had a stroke. We have to wait and see. The next twenty-four hours are very important." He took a deep breath. "I'll take you girls home, then come back here."

"I need to see her," Brenda said.

"We can't right now. She's in intensive care," Larry said.

24

"I've got to see with my own eyes that she's not dead," Brenda said loudly.

"But, Brenda–"

"I'm not leaving until I see her." Brenda crossed her arms and sat back in the chair.

A doctor pulled Larry aside. After they talked, Larry waved the girls over. "The doctor said you can see her for one minute. That's all. Even though she's unconscious she can still hear us, so no tears. Okay?"

"Okay," they both said at the same time.

All three followed a nurse to the intensive care ward. "Only two at a time," she said.

"You girls go ahead. I'll wait here," Larry said.

After they put on a gown and mask, the nurse took them to her bed. "Just one minute," she said, pulling the curtain around the bed.

"Grandmom?" Brenda whispered.

She was hooked up to all kinds of tubes and monitors. A wall of machines blinked and beeped on the other side of the bed. The air was a suffocating blanket of pine cleaner and ammonia.

Brenda reached through the wires and tubes to touch her face. "I love you, Grandmom."

"Me too," Angelique said, caressing the back of her hand. "We saw the snakes. We're going to make a special gris-gris for you. To help you get better."

Brenda looked at Angelique, then back at her grandmother. "We'll make the best healing gris-gris ever when we get back to the house."

Her eyelids fluttered, but her eyes didn't open.

"Stay with us, Grandmom," Brenda said.

The nurse pulled the curtain open. "We have to let her rest now, girls."

Outside the room, Larry said, "Let's get you two home."

Once they were back at the house, Larry said, "Call me on my cell phone if you need anything. I'll be back in a few hours. Will you be all right by yourself? I can have someone look in on you."

"Daddy, we'll be fine. Go ahead." Brenda gave him a hug and kiss.

"We'll take care of each other," Angelique said, hugging him.

After he got in the car and drove away, the girls ran to their bedroom. Brenda emptied her box onto the bed.

"Do you think it's Mrs. Johnston doing bad magic against Grandmom?" Angelique asked.

"Maybe, if somewhere in her crazy mind she decided Grandmom had done something against her. I can't imagine anyone else wanting to hurt her," Brenda spread out the ribbons, rocks and pieces of glass and metal from the box.

"This is all junk." She took a handful and threw it onto her pillow. "Nothing good enough to help her."

"Then we've got to find better things. Grandmom must have good stuff in her room, don't you think?" Angelique asked.

"Yes, but–"

"We're doing this for her." Angelique grabbed Brenda's arm. "Come on."

They entered her bedroom. A sweet scent, like roses, filled the air. Brenda pulled the thick, white curtains closed and turned on the light. Angelique stood near the dark wood bed. There was a hot ripple in the air, like the wake of a boat in water. "Do you feel that?"

Brenda lifted her hand to the air. "Yes." An edge of blue suede peeked out from under the bed. "What is this?" Brenda picked up the small bag. "Grandmom's nation bag. She always carries it. Why would she leave it here?"

"I don't know." Angelique laid the bag on the middle of the bed. "But maybe we can use it."

Angelique opened the closet and mix of earthy scents floated into the air. They found a wood cabinet in the closet with jars and boxes of herbs, roots, and powder.

"This is strong magic stuff," Brenda said.

"Good. That's what we need."

"This is too much for us." Brenda backed out of the closet.

Angelique grabbed Brenda's arm. "We can't have any doubt. You taught me that." Angelique slowly moved her open hands over the containers, letting her light guide her. She kept the image of her grandmother healthy in her mind. When the center of her palm tingled intensely she picked up a jar. She handed three jars to Brenda.

One had the word 'John root' written on its label. The other two had designs drawn on their labels.

"We'll do it here." Angelique said.

"How do you know those are the right things?" Brenda said.

Angelique took her hand; they touched each item together. "You see. They feel right."

Brenda nodded.

"We need to do a spell of protection, then make the gris-gris. I'll be right back." Brenda rushed out of the room.

Angelique waited in the middle of the room. There was a quick movement in the corner. When she turned her head, there was nothing there. Each time she blinked something fluttered in the air, just out of her vision. Her heart beat faster. It took all her strength not to run out of the room. She opened her mouth to call Brenda, but closed her eyes instead. Whatever it was, it couldn't or wouldn't touch her.

She stood still until Brenda returned with a paper bag. Brenda emptied the bag on the floor. There were five different color candles, matches, chalk, a pair of scissors and a can of beer. She pulled a piece of red flannel and ribbon from her pocket.

"For the spell of protection," Brenda said. "Do you remember how it's made?"

Angelique nodded, took a pillow off the bed, placed it on the floor and put her grandmother's nation bag on the pillow. "This is Grandmom."

They drew a chalk circle around the pillow and placed the candles on the edge of the circle. Angelique opened one of the jars with a pattern on it and sprinkled a few grains of the black powder in between the candles.

"To keep her safe," Angelique said.

Brenda laid the six-inch square of red flannel on the floor. Angelique held a pen over the material without touching it, then after a few seconds drew a pattern on the material. Brenda wrote their grandmother's name nine times on a piece of paper. Angelique laid a piece of John root in the paper, sprinkled the brown powder from the other jar on it and folded the paper up. They tied it close; each took turns tying a knot in the ribbon.

Brenda opened the beer. Angelique dipped her finger in the can and dripped beer on the gris-gris to feed it. They placed it on the pillow next to the nation bag. Brenda lit the candles while her cousin dribbled a little beer in her hands and threw it in each corner of the room. They sat on the floor, held hands and watched the candles burn. Shadows slid and jumped in the corners like trapped animals.

"Whatever you are, you have to leave this house," Angelique said.

Shadows crawled up the walls. The candles' flames jerked back and forth. A crunching sound, like mice chewing paper came from under the bed. Brenda peeked under the bed, but saw nothing.

"It's time to go away and leave our Grandmother alone." Brenda pushed light from deep inside. Warm yellow light, like melted butter, dripped from her hands and feet.

Angelique saw Brenda's light and gathered stillness inside and pushed out. Gold light from her hands and feet mixed with Brenda's light and pooled on the floor around them. They stared at the candles.

Their light streamed to the dark corners. Obscure shapes twisted up the wall, away from the girls' light.

A giggle snapped in the air above them. They looked up for one second, into each other's eyes. In a blink, they were sitting in a field of daisies. A warm summer breeze bounced over the flowers and caressed their faces. The setting sun filled the sky with streaks of blue, purple and white.

They were two other girls, holding one flower. They took turns pulling a petal off.

"He loves me," one girl sang.

"He loves me," the other girl chanted back.

When the last petal was pulled the girls fell into each other's arms laughing.

Angelique and Brenda plummeted through a dark tunnel and were back in their Grandmother's bedroom.

"What — what was that?" Angelique asked, gulping for air.

"I think that was Grandmom and — " Brenda shuddered. " — and Mrs. Johnston."

"How could that be?" Angelique asked.

"I don't know. Grandmom never said anything about them knowing each other when they were younger. Maybe it's a trick."

Angelique shook her head. "That felt true. Something happened between them, something that made her hate Grandmom."

"I don't care what happened. I won't lose Grandmom," Brenda said. "Look– they're coming back. This was just something to stop us."

The shadow things had leaked back down the walls as the girls' light dissipated.

"No more tricks, true or not." Brenda concentrated on the candles again. She took deep, slow breaths to calm down.

Angelique held Brenda's hands and did the same. The light flowed again from them, at first in a steady stream and then a rushing torrent as they kept one purpose in mind: to rescue their grandmother. Sounds echoed above them: giggles, singing, small feet jumping up and down. No matter what they heard they kept their eyes on the dancing flames. Gold light filled the floor and lapped up the walls. They didn't even look up when the crying started, a little girl wailing deeply.

The shadows on the ceiling curled in on themselves, wept down the walls to the floor and faded away. The girls watched the candles burn until they were so tired they couldn't keep their eyes open. The shadows and sounds didn't return.

"It's gone." Angelique put out the candles. "We'll take the gris-gris and nation bag to her tomorrow."

Calm quiet surrounded them. Brenda nodded.

They put the pillow back, picked up the candles, swept the powder and chalk into the paper bag, and went back to their room. Too tired to eat, they fell asleep and didn't hear Larry come in.

He woke them in the morning to take them to the hospital.

Once there, the doctor told them that she was out of intensive care but still being watched. She hadn't regained consciousness, but her vital signs were stable. The girls looked at each other, smiling.

The nurse took the girls to her room while Larry talked to the doctor.

She wasn't hooked up to as many machines as the day before. Brenda kissed her hand.

"We made a gris-gris for you, Grandmom. Angelique and I did it together."

Angelique took the charm out of her pocket, placed it in her grandmother's left hand, and held it.

"And we found your nation bag." Brenda placed the bag in her grandmother's right hand. "We did the biggest magic we knew, Grandmom."

"We did it because we love you and want you back," Angelique said.

Brenda jumped. "She squeezed my hand."

Their grandmother's eyes opened and she smiled.

Brenda leaned forward to hug her, but stopped as another face floated over their grandmother's face.

"You my girls, my shiny light," a familiar voice said.

The face smiled with broken teeth.

"Get out!" Brenda said, trying to pull away from her tight grip.

Mrs. Johnston laughed. "Why should I? You play, let me in. I'm staying now. You mine."

"Oh no." Angelique said. She finally saw how this happened. The magic they practiced in the house must have made an opening in Grandmom's protection. "It was us. We let her in."

Horror flashed on Brenda's face.

"No!" Brenda said. Light shot out of her free hand and poured over Grandmom.

"That's right, give me your light, my shiny key."

Angelique pushed light out of her hands but none came out.

"Not yet, my sweet. Later, there'll be time for you and me later," the face over Grandmom's said.

Angelique's light and voice was locked inside. She could do nothing except watch Mrs. Johnston absorb Brenda's light. The old woman's body laid over their grandmother's like a gelatinous blanket, getting thicker each second.

"Grandmom, help me," Brenda whispered, stumbling against the bed.

"She can't help you now. I got her nice and tight. Soon she be gone, then we have a good time," Mrs. Johnston said, her body filling out, the spectral skin stretching.

Angelique prayed inside, wanting to close her eyes, but could not.

Brenda's lips moved, but no sounds came out, tears streamed down her face.

"Mommy," Brenda blurted out. The gold light traveling from her to Mrs. Johnston turned lighter in color; green light streaked its edges. Brenda suddenly remembered a picture of her mother in a silk gown that same color green. It was her mother's favorite color.

"Help me, Mommy."

"Stop that." Mrs. Johnston twisted back and forth as the green light increased, pulling from Brenda's arms and chest. "Stop, stop, stop..." Her body inflated larger like a balloon.

Angelique snapped loose from her control, and staggered away from the bed. When she took a step towards Brenda, a soft voice whispered in her ear, 'wait'. Angelique took one step towards Brenda. The voice pleaded gently, 'stay here, it will be alright'. The voice was like her mother's but softer. In her heart she could feel it wasn't Mrs. Johnston. Brenda stood taller, her eyes closed, her mouth moving silently as if she was calmly talking to someone.

The outline of Mrs. Johnston's body thinned as the green light filled her form and spiked out in fine lines to the walls. She changed into a two-headed dog, but still the light stabbed through her, the dog's mouth open in an unuttered howl. A huge snake coiled over their grandmother's body, the light slicing through it in rings. The snake shape changed into a gigantic bird, snapping at the lines of light penetrating its body. No matter what she became the green light continued eating holes in her form. Mrs. Johnston returned to a human shape, slowly deflating.

"You shoulda been mine," she said in a tiny voice, before the aspect of her body slid to the floor and disappeared.

Angelique ran to Brenda, catching her as she wobbled against the bed. A sheen of sweat covered Brenda's face. "Mommy?" she asked.

"You did it, Brenda, you made her go away," Angelique said.

"It wasn't me."

A moan from the bed made them turn towards their grandmother.

Her eyes flickered open. "Brenda, honey," she said slowly.

"Grandmom," they both said, hugging her.

"How?" she asked.

"I've been studying online," Brenda said. "I taught Angelique what I know. And she taught me some things I didn't know last night."

"I should have guessed there was too much Power between the two of you to ignore," Grandmom said.

"It was Mrs. Johnston, she used us to get to you," Brenda said. "But Mommy helped us push her away."

"Oh, my babies. You didn't know what you were doing." She shook her head. "They found Shelia's body in her house, two weeks ago. She'd been dead a long time. I didn't want upset you."

"Shelia is Mrs. Johnston? You knew each other when you were young?" Brenda asked.

Their grandmother closed her eyes for a moment. She squeezed their hands and looked at them. "Yes. We were like sisters once, but a man drove us apart." She shook her head. "Love can be a tricky thing. Or lust." She held their hands over her heart. "Don't let that happen to you."

"No, Grandmom, never," Angelique said, taking Brenda's other hand.

"No one will come between us," Brenda said.

The doctor and Larry walked into the room. Larry ran to the bed and hugged her and the girls. "I knew you were too strong to let anything keep you down," he said.

"The hugs can continue in a few minutes, but I need to check my patient," the doctor said. "Could you wait outside?"

"Make it fast, because I've got a lot of work to do at home," Grandmom said. She slipped the nation bag back to Brenda and the gris-gris to Angelique.

The doctor and Larry walked through the green and gold light that splashed and shimmered in the room without seeing it. Brenda and Angelique waved to their Grandmother from the doorway, knowing she was safe now, surrounded by the power.

Forever Dead

I was happy before I became a zombie
    stumbling through Central Park at night
sleeping in a tumble of fallen trees all day.

Memories of my past life jumble together
    best forgotten when I lie
face down in ripe yielding earth.

I was happy before I lost my soul
    to the will of a Voodoo Goddess
binding me to the light in her eyes.

Dreams do not come but if they could
    they would be of dying once
falling forever into pure stillness.

369 Gates of Hell

The Gate of Impending Irrevocability:

Redi Thomas had spent Friday afternoon alone in the reception area of the office building. She'd been bodyguard to Ana Sanchez, an accountant to some of the richest musicians in the business, for two months. There wasn't much to look at between the wood paneling and plush black leather furniture, besides a huge bowl of dried flowers on the silver center table, and the ghosts.

Two men and a woman. The female ghost kept her back to Redi, exposing her open skull. Her curly brown hair framed the ragged hole. The two males' heads flopped back every now and then to expose their cut throats. Blood flowed endlessly from the neck wounds, cascading around them to soak into the white carpet. Redi remembered killing them.

"Useless haunting, guys," she whispered. "I can't hear you and I've seen this before." She leaned over the silver table and used the reflection to pat her short afro into shape and put lip gloss on. Carrying a mirror to freshen up wasn't her style but her client always looked good so Redi tried to be as presentable as possible. Dressed as usual in black, Redi's turtle neck covered the old scars; the jacket covered her gun and holster. No one would mistake her for pretty, but her high cheek bones and naturally plump lips had attracted more than one man or woman.

Ana came out of her office carrying her overstuffed briefcase, Armani pantsuit still looking crisp. She pushed her straight red hair behind her ears, and nodded to Redi. They walked to the elevator and Ana used her thumbprint to activate the private elevator.

Redi's tall frame cast a shadow over the petite accountant as they waited for the elevator. She tracked both ends of the hallway in peripheral vision. There was no movement except for the thin images of the ghosts nearby.

The elevator stopped in the parking garage. The white limousine waited for them near the elevator. Suddenly, there was a low growl behind Redi, and the sound of a large animal's claws scraping the concrete. Without turning, Redi shoved Ana in the limo and jumped in behind her, drawing the small gun from a shoulder holster.

"What are you doing?" the accountant asked.

Redi looked through the side and back tinted windows to the empty garage. "You didn't hear anything?"

Ana straightened her suit. "Not a thing."

"I heard something, maybe a large dog," Redi said, putting the gun away. She tapped on the glass between them and the driver to signal they could go. Whatever had been there, it was gone now.

When they arrived at Ana's apartment building, she said to Redi, "It's a good thing it's Friday. You need to get some rest this weekend. I don't need a jumpy bodyguard."

Redi nodded and watched her enter the building.

The ghosts followed her down the street and into the subway. She waited on the subway platform at the right end furthest from the Friday night crowd.

"What do you think is happening?" she asked them softly.

The female ghost spun wildly. Glowing bits of her smashed brain disappeared into the shadows. The male ghosts made faces at Redi while taking turns on their knees pounding the concrete platform and trying to tear at her with their hands.

"No opinion?" She could use a cigarette, but the vibration under her feet and a gentle push of air signaled her train coming.

The streets of the Lower East Side were filled with people on their way to dinner, mostly innocents, although she didn't believe in innocence. The others, pickpockets, drug dealers, gang members, and desperate people, were sprinkled among the crowd. Only the most dangerous dared to make eye contact with Redi. They nodded respectfully when she looked in their direction.

As soon as she unlocked her building door, the three ghosts flitted away. She sighed. That meant there would be different ghosts waiting in her apartment. They had started following her three years ago, when she changed careers. It was ironic that they showed up after she stopped being a hired assassin.

Midway up the second flight of the creaky wooden stairs, she heard the growl again. Redi took her gun out and stood in a shadowed corner of the hallway. The sound of claws slamming the stairs sped up as the large animal began to run.

She clicked off the safety and waited. The growls were deafening. Unable to stand it any longer, Redi ran to the edge of the stairwell and leaned over the banister pointing her gun down. . . at nothing.

Leaning back against the wall, she took a deep breath. Either she was losing her mind, or someone was playing an elaborate trick. Someone with a death wish, because this wasn't even mildly amusing. She walked up to the third floor with her gun in her right hand, unlocked her apartment door, turned off the alarm and locked the door behind her.

She flipped on the light. Movement in the center of the living room made her swing the gun with two hands at a huge two-headed gray and white wolf. It stood almost as tall as Redi in front of her red leather couch, both heads growling. She aimed for its heart.

"Sh-h-h, Geh, sit down," a male voice said from Redi's right. The animal crouched on the floor, low growls still echoing from its twin throats, two pairs of red eyes fixed on Redi.

She spun around and pointed the gun at a slim, tall man leaning against the wall with his arms crossed. He was dressed in a white tuxedo; his long wavy dark hair almost touched the floor. His features were Japanese, but his skin was mocha brown, the same shade as Redi's. She thought he had no eyes, but realized they were entirely black. She could see the wall through him.

Some kind of ghost, but not anyone she had killed.

"Who are you?" she asked, putting the gun down on the ebony wood coffee table.

He smiled, showing stained pointed teeth. "I need a favor."

"I don't do that kind of work anymore," Redi said, pouring gin into a glass. "What would you offer me to come out of retirement, a shot at redemption?"

She lit a cigarette, inhaled slowly and sat down on the couch. He sat opposite her, but not on anything she could see. The dog lay at his feet, its huge heads surrounded by blue flames.

He shook his head. "That only happens in the movies."

"Then why should I do this favor for you?"

He uncrossed his long legs and leaned forward.

"After all you've done," he said, spreading long fingers out, the three-inch nails shaped to needle points. "What would removing one more person from this time and space mean?"

"It occurs to me, looking at you, that one more person just might mean the difference between one level of hell and another," she said.

"You've got to know that, with your body count, there's not much to hope for when you die," he said, waving around the room.

The room filled with ghosts, the silent kind that Redi was used to seeing. Usually there were only a few at a time, now they crowded the room. They watched, a few laughed silently and pointed.

"So I kill this one person for you and get what in return?" she asked.

He stood and walked through ebony wood coffee table. The dog rolled over onto its side. "I could get you a few hours a day without the company of your victims."

"I've gotten used to being followed by ghosts." She reached through his leg to set her glass down on the coffee table. "I'm sure there's somebody else you could get to kill this person for you," she said, putting her feet up on the coffee table.

Linda Addison

The ghost paced back and forth in front of her, his long hair streamed behind him as if floating through water.

"I can't say why right now, but you have to be the one," he said.

Redi leaned forward, took a drink. "Hmmm, let me take a guess. I'm in so deep that one killing won't really affect my, let's call it, Karma?"

"Actually killing this person is going to be good for you. Get you one step closer to your true destiny." He stopped pacing and sat down again in the air. The dog sat up and raised its heads. One stared at Redi, the other at the ghost.

"My destiny? What the hell does that mean?" she asked.

"Hell indeed." He smiled.

Redi stared at him. "You seem familiar, but I don't remember you being one of my hits," she said, pointing her cigarette at him.

The dog barked. The ghost glared at it. "We — uh — worked together. You didn't kill me."

"I always work alone," she said, narrowing her eyes.

He closed his eyes as if he was listening to something, and then looked at her, "We have — had a very special relationship. I can't say any more about our association at this time."

"It's hard to imagine I would have forgotten you," Redi said.

"In time you will remember me and much more. Trauma can make it necessary for the mind to veil certain... events until the time is right."

A flash of her stepfather's face and the smell of burning flesh made her stomach twist. The thick scar tissue on her back itched at the memory. "Who is this person that you want killed?" she asked.

"You'll get all the details when you agree to do it," he said.

Redi looked around the room. There were more ghosts there than ever before. All people she had killed, including the occasional dog or cat, pets of her hits that starved to death. She sighed.

"You're right, one more dead person isn't a big deal," she said, grounding out the cigarette in a brass ashtray. "Here's the thing, I need more incentive if I'm going to add to my entourage."

He closed his eyes again and pressed on his temples with fingers so long they looked like they had an extra joint.

"Okay," he said. "I can offer you revenge against your stepfather."

She jerked back on the couch. "He's dead."

He waved his hand dismissively. "I have access to his essence. I can choose to interrupt his eternal suffering so you can have some quality time with him."

"You're more than a ghost, aren't you?" she asked.

He nodded.

"Are you the Devil?"

He laughed. "No, but you might say I'm second-in-command."

Redi stood up and walked to the window overlooking her busy street. "Can I have time to think about your offer?" She turned to face him.

He pressed in close. She held her ground. A stench of burning flesh surrounded him. "One night."

She thought for a second that he was going to kiss her, but he inhaled deeply as though breathing in her scent, and turned quickly.

The two-headed dog rose and followed him across the room.

"Sleep well, Redi Thomas." He snapped his fingers and all the other ghosts disappeared. He smiled at her, bowed and sank through the floor with the dog.

She leaned against the wall and looked at the room, the empty room. It had been so long since she had been alone here. Perhaps she could sleep without nightmares this one night.

The Gate of Relentless Congruity:

Redi sipped her second cup of coffee and lit another cigarette. She had one dream last night. The one recurring train dream she'd had for years. The conductor was a pale, bloated man with black eyes and a belt of keys. The dream ended as it always did, with her and the conductor working on her stepfather while he was tied to a table in one of the train cars.

She smiled at the memory of his imagined screams.

The talking ghost rose through the floor with his dog. "We can make him scream together," he said, sitting down opposite her. The dog walked over to Redi and sniffed her with its twin heads, whined and sat on the floor.

Redi thought she heard a whisper under the dog's whine, but couldn't make out the words. "Okay. Who do you want me to kill?"

Ana Sanchez, the accountant. Redi should have known it wasn't going to be a stranger. She had nothing against the woman, but her feelings or lack of feelings for a hit had never stopped her from completing a contract in the past.

"I'll have to leave town, change identities," she said. "No one will hire a bodyguard with a dead client."

"Do what you need, but it must be done this weekend and — "

"I got it the first time, leave her body where her family will find it," she said. He smiled widely.

"I do this and I get to make him suffer?" she asked.

"Oh, we don't have to wait. Your word is good enough. Let's take that train ride." He leaned close to her, his hand brushed her face. Redi didn't feel his hand but there was a jolt of scalding air on her skin. She closed her eyes.

Clanging metal jolted Redi upright in her seat, her knees bumping against the back of a train seat. The clink of heavy chains and metal tools jostling against each other sang out from under the conductor's long blue coat as he walked down the aisle. His mouth was a dark wound in a pasty face, his eyes two shadows under the ledge of his cap.

As soon as he left Redi quickly moved to the exit in front of the car and punched the door panel. She walked through the opening and took the passageway in two quick jumps. The next car door wouldn't open. She looked through its tiny window. A dark curtain blocked the view.

The conductor was suddenly behind her. He wrapped his arm around her neck. She kicked and elbowed him but his steel grip never loosened. He squeezed until she slipped into unconsciousness.

Redi woke strapped to a metal table under a circle of bright light. A rubber sheet covered her naked body. As she struggled against the leather straps a familiar voice asked, "Are you so reluctant to accept your reward?"

"This isn't what we agreed on." She twisted her head to locate the speaker in the dark shadows of the train car.

A man wearing a long blue conductor's coat walked into the circle of light surrounding the table. It was the ghost she'd made a deal with. His eyes were completely white here.

"Now, let's see the whole picture." He pulled the rubber sheet off her naked body. Old scars lay in patterns across her chest, stomach and legs. The burn scars on her back were a thick pad against the metal table. "Your stepfather was a meticulous man."

"What are you doing?" she asked, shuddering.

"I'm honoring our agreement." He gently traced a scar on her stomach with his fingernail. His touch was light as butterfly wings. "I'm pleased to be able to provide you what you require."

"I didn't ask for this," she screamed, kicking in spite of the restraints. Bones in her ankles cracked.

He opened his coat to reveal shiny surgical tools interlaced in the brown skin of his chest.

The leather straps bit into her wrists and ankles as she thrashed back and forth. Animal sounds rose from her chest, erupting into deep shrieks. She bit her tongue; blood mixed with spit as she screamed and growled at him.

He waited until her energy was gone and she collapsed onto the metal table. Then he slowly pulled a slim, hook-shaped scalpel from his chest.

"Please, don't..." she said in a small, hoarse voice.

He leaned close to her face. A sweet scent made her stomach churn; it was the cologne her stepfather wore. It took all her strength not to vomit. The ghost laid the cold metal tool on her convulsing stomach. "Look." He pointed across the room.

A light turned on the opposite wall of the train car. Invisible bonds against the padded wall held her stepfather. He started whimpering.

The ghost held her head up and picked the scalpel up with his other hand. He used the blunt side to trace a long 'Z' shaped scar that crossed her belly. Burning slid deep from inside her and out through the scar. A childhood of fear and deep rage began to boil away. She moaned. Her stepfather screamed as his stomach opened at the middle; thick black liquid bubbled out. Her scar disappeared.

The ghost rubbed hot fingers over the re-smoothed skin. "This will take a while. Watch closely."

He worked slowly. Her stepfather screamed and begged as his body gathered fresh wounds. Redi studied how each instrument was used. When her scars were gone, he released her from the table and they worked together on her stepfather to create new wounds.

Hours seemed to pass and Redi didn't tire. What was left when he finally stopped screaming didn't resemble a human as much as a dissection diagram.

Redi opened her eyes. She was still sitting at the kitchen table opposite the ghost. The clock over the stove showed about the same time.

"What kind of trick was that?" she asked, throwing the coffee cup at the ghost. The ceramic mug passed through him and shattered against the wall.

"No trick," he said, opening his hands as if to show he had nothing up his sleeves. "Look." He pointed to her chest.

She lifted her t-shirt. The scars were gone. She jumped up and ran to the bedroom and looked at the brown smooth skin on her back and legs. All the scars were gone.

He stood in the doorway. "What do you feel inside when you think of him?"

The deep twisting bitterness was gone. Nightmare memories no longer burned in her gut. She sat down on the bed, picked up a cigarette, looked at it and put it down.

"Is this real?" she asked, tears in her eyes. All the hatred, disregard for human life, disbelief in anything good was gone. The pain of all the people she had killed overwhelmed her, she ran to the sink to vomit. Redi asked, "How did you do this?"

The ghost shrugged. "Bodies are illusionary fragments of flesh. This body is in this reality, so this is real. In another realm things could be very different."

"You like to talk in riddles, don't you?" she said, wiping away tears.

He smiled. "I assume you can still do your part, even without your deep-seated, unresolved anger?" he asked, standing.

Redi closed her eyes. "Yes, I can." She picked up the cigarette and lit it. "I'll need some time alone."

"Indeed." He bowed and melted into the floor with the dog.

The Gate of Descending Reversion:

Redi shaved her head, dressed in black jeans, and shirt. She pulled a dark leather jacket out of the back of her closet. The black felt hat fit snugly. The wide brim cast a deep shadow over her face.

She entered Ana's building at midnight. The apartment building was easy to get in since Redi knew where the secured entrances were and how to open them, information necessary to protect her client.

Cutting the lines to the security cameras was just as easy. The lock to Ana's apartment wasn't much of a challenge. The entryway in the large apartment was dimly lit. The bedrooms were down the hall to the left. The light was on in Ana's office to the right of the living room. Redi leaned against the hallway wall listening to the accountant type on the computer.

She stood in the shadow of the hall for a long time. She had never felt before how connected one human life was to so many others: Ana's son, husband, clients, relatives and friends. This woman was loved and needed by others. Her death would cause so much pain. As much as Redi didn't want to kill her, she couldn't return to the soulless person she had been.

Redi used a silencer so Ana's son wouldn't wake up. She dragged Ana's body to the middle of the living room.

The accountant's husband was supposed to be out of town. Redi had no idea they kept a gun in the apartment. She took two bullets in the back but managed to get out of the apartment after rushing him. He put another bullet in her upper right arm before she knocked him out.

Redi stumbled up the emergency stairs to the roof and collapsed against the air conditioning tower. Dark blood pooled around her in a slowly widening circle.

Redi had few breaths left. The ghost and his dog appeared between breaths.

"Come to collect my soul?" she asked, with a strained smile.

He bent near her face. The scent of burning flesh was surprisingly comforting to Redi. The dog laid both heads in her lap. She could feel their weight.

"I've come to help you remember your destiny, as I always have before," he said.

"I don't have time for your word games," she said through clenched teeth.

"This game is done. You're very close to the last Gate, and returning to me and where you belong."

The dog's heads were heavier on her lap. Redi shook her head and coughed blood. "Last gate?"

He leaned close to her face. His tongue flicked out and wet the inside of her right ear.

Her true identity crashed back into her mind. She was infinitely more than the cells of this dying body, had lived longer than documented history. She arched her back, trying to stand up as the truth of her existence filled the dying meat brain.

He held her hand as she collapsed back to the ground.

"Show me," she growled, pulling his face close to hers.

Thick dark light poured from his eyes over her face. She drank the bitter darkness in her open mouth. The memories of the other mortal lives she'd suffered through came into crisp focus.

"Dearest Abaddon, which Gate am I passing through now?" she asked.

"The Gate of Emanating Reconstruction, Magnificent Ender of Light," he said, tears of blood dripping from his eyes onto his white tuxedo.

The dog whimpered.

"It's good to see you again also, Geh." She shifted her weight, causing waves of pain to pulse through her back. "How're things below?"

"The maintenance of the tortured is arduous, but the torment continues, as you would want, Most Fantastic Being. I miss you dearly." He leaned forward on his knees to support her head. "Has your pain been all you wished?" he asked.

She closed her eyes. "Oh, yes," she whispered. "Your healing my pain made the last killing particularly difficult."

He kissed her hand. "We're pleased to do anything for you, Deliverer of Exquisite Pain."

She moaned. "I'm ready to return to work. It's been enlightening to see the job from the other point of view. See you soon." She slumped to the ground.

Abaddon sniffed the body to be sure there was no life left. The dog stood, walked around the body nine times, and howled.

Linda Addison

Bottling Up De Evil

De glass bottles
    blue, green, yellow
gathered by the faithful.

Mama Earth feeds the trees
    roots sunk deep
sweet tender pale fingers.

Reaching into the sky
    red cedar arms
slender tips covered in glass.

De bottle trees
    trapping flying spirits
holding them tight.

Until the night wind comes
    bringing the clinking moans
ending only with the morning.

It is the new light
    bringing deliverance
to lost and hungry souls.

Night of the Living and Dead

They started early this year. The sun had barely set as she watched the flickering lights through the thick fog over the cemetery. Loud music and yelling thumped in the air. Her youngest one began to whimper.

"Don't cry, baby," she said, caressing his head.

"The lights are scary," he whined. "Are they going to make those noises all night like last year?"

She stared through the thick fog at the lights again and shook her head. The sound of loud voices mixed with haunting music. "I don't know, but you need your rest, honey. We have to try to ignore them."

"Why do they do this every year?" her oldest asked.

"Something disturbs them at this time of the year," she said. "Perhaps the end of summer and the beginning of winter wakes something strange in them. We just have to stay put and wait for the night to end. They won't bother us."

"But what will we do if they come out here?"

"They won't," she tried to sound calm, but she could see shadows moving in the oddly lit fog. She suppressed a shudder.

"Come, babies, time to rest. We'll get through this night and then we'll have a year of quiet before we have to worry about them again." She turned her back to the pulsing sounds and gently pushed them ahead.

"In you go," she said, kissing them as they lay down.

"You won't let them get us?" the youngest whimpered.

"No, baby," she said. "I'll be near you as usual." She covered them both and slowly lowered her aching bones into her grave, willed the dirt into place, and tried not to think about the sounds coming from the Halloween party in the house across the street from the cemetery.

Alien Bathroom

The Zirk's top scientists
    turned their kata twice to the left
jumped up and down three times
    and said the sanu mantra.

The Vanuta's top priestess
    burned emsnu incense
sacrificed a many-noodled cangi
    and slithered across the ancient floor.

All fifty thousand Kirsx hive members
    danced the rhythmic dance of death
for ten cycles of their moon
    and promptly fell asleep.

The remaining archaeologists
    argued to blows over the object
until a minor Gorkling pulled the shiny stick
    and the toilet flushed.

Excerpts from The Unabridged Traveler's Guide as UFOs in Galaxy A.G.2

Chapter 3, Section 1.3.1a:

Maintain an acceptable holo image at all times when visiting the most interesting planet, native-named Earth, in the "Milky Way" galaxy. Neatness and a good fitting image will gain high marks on the believability scale if inadvertently seen by Earth's sentient beings. Several varieties of images have been tested and rated in this galaxy. Certain highly stylized images have been found to invoke agitated states in members of the species. Reference: "Mars Attacks" vid 84.I.77, "Alien" vid series 39.N.5.2.

However, there is a wide range of acceptable non-Earth styles to choose from that allow individuality and personal style. Simplicity within the seeded archetypes has found to be most successful. For popular interpretations of these images reference: "Close Encounters of the Third Kind" vid 45.A.3.7, "X-Files" vid series 849.N.4.9.

An exception to the lists of fashionable images is the favorite earthling Elvis look. A minimal amount of language and behavior imprinting is necessary to become acceptable to the natives. The only restriction is for travelers sensitive to flash light, since this look invokes picture taking from the natives. This image will allow you to travel among the natives freely; however, it is important to keep in mind that this look should only be worn in the Las Vegas sector, to avoid the rippling effects that have resulted from its overuse. See references to multi-media archives, keyword: "Elvis Sightings".

Chapter 7, Section 5.2.9g:

Abduction of human beings has been strictly forbidden since the unfortunate incidents with unconscious memory leaks. These leaks have not caused any high level problems and the long term effects have been entertaining; however, they introduce unacceptable risks for the travel program. Reference: all works of Chris Carter starting in the 20th Century vid series 209.Z.4.7.

Abduction of other life forms is allowed as long as the entire creature is taken. Although the problems produced by the Geuu taking only internal organs and leaving the external coverings (see section on Bovine Internal Studies) has not resulted in Earth being put on the non-visitor list, we do not want to create additional issues for the Interspatial Uniplacated Traveler's Board (IUTB).

Chapter 14, Section 8.4.2v:

It is important to establish viable landing sites if planet fall is intended. Studies have found that locations of expected visitation are best since the local natives will have already woven tales to explain any signs of other worldly sightings. Reference maps of Roswell, Grovers Mill, Area 51. Other sectors have been deemed attractive because of their tolerance of aberrant images. Reference layouts of Hollywood, New York City, all locations of Disney World.

When visiting Earth it is important to clean up after yourself. The non-littering clause signed by all participants of the traveler's contract will be strictly enforced. Dark matter, hot or cold, in particular must be kept out of this developing galaxy for obvious reasons. Manipulation of native material is strictly forbidden from the sub-molecular level to larger structures. Documented incidents of the breaking of these rules serve as clear examples of what not to do, no matter how visually pleasing. Reference: the Step Pyramid of King Joser in Egypt, which involved the masterful memory imprinting of several generations of natives. Note that the creation of crop circles by vacationers is discouraged unless you hold at least a Level III certificate in topical soil and plant design. Although amusing in its final result, these kinds of graffiti will no longer be tolerated by IUTB.

In conclusion, we expect all vacationers to review the entire Traveler's Guide in any preferred form (visual, eatable, scent, spiked, etc) and commit it to memory. Enjoy!

Pullus Cogens

It stood on the edge
    after calculating Rolm's Levels of Acceleration,
while considering circular argumentation
    of the Newtonian principles of inertia,
the displacement of the Aristotelian assumption
    of natural place.

It mulled over the possibility of a glitch
    in the inverse-square law,
the use of translational motion over
    rotational motion meant only one thing,
it had to cross the road
    to get to the other side.

Linda Addison

One Night at Sheri-Too-Long's Popcorn Bar

"This is a very special day," he says, raising his glass with his six fingered third hand and tapping my glass.

Why does this always happen to me? I could go to the loneliest, faraway bar — a place on a planet outside the known universe and some unnamed genetic hybrid will find me. They always treat me like a long lost brother. They talk and talk and talk until I'm all sticky and wet with their words.

I discreetly blink a change control code into my three-dimensional self-projector implant to create a transformation in my outer displacement.

"I'm a lucky guy!" he says smiling, looking straight into my eyes.

So transparency doesn't bother this guy. Great. I fade back into the bar's temporal zone just in time for the bartender('s hair) to notice me. Her dark cloak of hair undulates around her body, covering her in a living full-length gown.

A mass of curls form '??' above her head. I draw '==' on the counter and longingly watch her hair make another Ankle-high Buffalo Bill for me while the bartender carries on a conversation in sign language with a Venusian in a pressurized tank. I begin to imagine what else hair like that could do...

"Not only is this a special day, but meeting you here really makes it unforgettable," he says.

The remnants of my daydreams scatter to the darker corners of the darkened bar. This guy has to pick now to get friendly. Just when I'm in the process of building up the energy to talk to the bartender; her hair's been giving me erotic daydreams all evening. I was definitely not looking for a pal, I want the bartender('s hair).

"Do I know you?" I ask as rudely as I can. I look him up and down. Didn't anyone tell him that polka dots were out of style on this side of the universe and those big, floppy red shoes — where did this guy come from?

"I know you're here, you know I'm here. Double knowing. It doesn't get better than this," he says confidently, his orange curly hair bobbing up and down as he nods.

Now I know I'm in trouble. I have no idea what he's talking about. So I just stare at him. Then suddenly his words have a startling affect on my subconscious, resulting in an unexpected physical change. I liquefy and pour into the rim around

48

the bar chair.

Wet.

I knew that was coming.

"You're my kind of person," he says and pours into his chair's rim. A drop splashes into me and suddenly we're in direct pipeline mental contact.

All matters of fellowship and love floods my mind. Life is good. Rainbows always come out after the rain. A list of words with a heart replacing the letter 'o' begins to march through my mind.

I recompose and say, "Just a minute — you can't just go around splashing yourself into strangers."

"I thought like that once," he says after recomposing. "But now that I've met you. Well, I can't stay unaffected. You're the best." He reaches out to slap me on the back, but I activate my Portable Matter Contact Repellent and his hand swings through a temporary tunnel in my torso.

That's my limit. Accidental mind drips are one thing (and I'm not so sure that drip was an accident), but body touching without so much as an eye-to-eye invitation — that's an outrage! I slide my right hand into my jacket searching for my Guiltless De-molecularizer when a thin filament wraps around my wrist. I look down and it's a strand of the bartender's hair. She's still talking to someone else, but her hair forms the words BE KIND in the air.

I can't believe it — a dream come true. Her hair noticed me! Maybe I could retrieve some joy from this evening. If...

If I could get rid of this guy and spend some time with the bartender('s hair). I take an empty hand out of my jacket and three strands of hair caress my cheek before the bartender walks to the other end of the bar. This gives me the kind of chills I've been fantasizing about since I first saw her hair in action.

It's time to jump to light speed. I have to make this guy go away and I have to do it in a civilized way since her hair made it clear it didn't want me to disperse him into star matter.

So this guy's sitting there real impressed with knowing me (I don't know why) and wanting something (I don't know what).

His eyes are bright and filled with expectation. I take all my three-dimensional energy, pipe it into a one-way line in his direction and say, "I can see that you want something — that you have a question to ask me."

He nods, smiling with a rim of pink teeth around his lower head. He looks around mischievously to see if anyone is listening and leans toward me.

I blink and his face had transforms to pasty white with blue eyebrows and a large, red, round nose.

"TRICK OR TREAT!" he yells. The force of his words flings me across the room and I adhere to the wall like one of those six pointed Niobium wall hangings.

Sticky.

Finally.

It is kind of a relief.

He runs out of the bar, laughing loudly. And it takes two hours for the bartender('s hair) to coax me down from the wall. Not the worst two hours of my life, but I'd rather have that kind of stuff done to me in private instead of in front of the gamey crowd of the bar. But sometimes you have to take your treats (or tricks) where you can get them.

Land Sharks

Designed as tiny harmless pets
    their escape from the genetic lab
was barely news worthy.

Cruising the concrete sidewalks
    their miniature fins bobbing up
through cracks in the grey squares.

Hoping for a tired pigeon or dropped food
    steering clear of leather soles
and running rubber cleats.

When death comes their tiny bodies
    lose form and meaning
becoming part of a crumbling sidewalk.

You might see a round grey pebble
    of an eye glint before it rolls over
to its rough concrete stomach.

Little Red in the Hood

"Lay another one on me, Goosie" she said, flicking the ashes from her cigarette across the bar into the ashtray next to the cash register. The scratched mirror over the bar reflected a perfect little girl, with curly hair, wearing a red velvet dress. Most of the usual crowd was missing, no doubt resting up for the evening ahead. It was Saturday, one of the busiest nights of the week.

"You really oughta slow down " The bartender pushed her wire frame glasses up on her nose and poured two fingers of vodka into Red's glass.

"Easy to say when it ain't you that's gotta go skipping through the same dark woods day after day only to end up in a wolf's belly," Red replied.

"Hey, kid," the wolf croaked from a small table in the corner, where he nursed a bottle of rum. "I've eaten better before I got stuck with this gig. At least you don't have to go through a c-section every night."

"Yeah, so am I supposed to feel better about getting dragged out of you?" She threw the cold, clear liquid to the back of her throat and shuddered. Smooth warmth filled her for a brief moment before the dusty, dank air of the bar cut back through her body.

"The Three Pigs tell me our hours might get cut back now that the Power Rangers are taking over," the wolf said.

"Yeah, yeah, I heard that same talk when that purple people eater was the in thing, but nothing changed. I'm not holding my breath waiting for those pastel freaks to change things."

"Things did slow down when Big Bird was topping the charts," Old MacDonald said two seats to her right.

"Those were good days," Red said softly, taking a drag on her cigarette. "We had time to hang out with Dorothy in the Green City, live a little. Now "

A screeching siren filled the air. A red light in the ceiling pulsed brightly. The siren stopped when two hulks dressed in green fatigues walked in. One jerked his finger at the girl and tossed her a bright red hooded cape. The other one gave the wolf the thumbs up. The wolf stood and limped towards the door.

"We've got a reading alert, bedtime stories starting on Grant Street. Let's go, and no trouble this time, girlie," the first one said.

"Come, my hairy one," she said, draping the cape over her shoulders and letting the wolf lean on her as they walked out the door. "Time to live happily ever after."

After I Ate the Apple

I saw colors a little bit different,
    edges of the garden came into focus,
I took a little walk – just to see what was out there
    I planned on coming back, really I did.

Found magic in my hands and my hips,
    found even a look could stir things up
so I stirred and stirred
    making little and big things.

With the walking my legs got stronger
    even with the calluses, I kept walking
making things bright and shiny, sweet and sour,
    I kept on stirring.

I planned to return, to show you what I found.
    Oh, there were so many things,
so much to stir up – keeping me busy,
    I forgot my way back.

Just Passing Through

Where was I?

((...))

Oh yeah, I was telling you when I first noticed I was changing.

I woke up Saturday morning feeling exhausted. The room spun. Throbbing pain crept across my forehead. I looked down at my hands and saw lights.

What — ?

((??))

Sparkling lights. Not fluorescent or 60 watt or halogen. I'm talking about infinite points of brightness in the brown flesh of my hands. In and on them.

If that wasn't bad enough my nicely manicured fingernails were no longer painted Pleasingly Plum. They had become little oval windows to outer space.

((!!))

I know it sounds strange, but this is what happened.

((...))

Apology accepted. And lay off the fancy titles. I'm not an official representative from Earth. Just call me Janet.

Anyway, no matter which way I turned my fingers all I saw was endless velvet darkness filled with sparkling stars.

((??))

Yes, every single finger. I thought it was those funny lights you see when you close your eyes and press on your eyeballs.

((...))

Oh. I forgot you don't have eyeballs.

((??))

Uh — yeah. I guess if I had anything like that and did that to them it might be the same. Then I looked down at my feet. They were transparent.

((??))

Like glass, but not shiny. I wiggled my toes. They felt normal but I could see the wood floor through them.

((??))

I did what any normal human would do. I closed my eyes. That didn't help because I could see through my eyelids.

The lights in my fingers grew into swirling intricate designs up my wrists and around my arms. That's when I first heard you.

((??))

No. Nothing like now. There was a low rumbling sweet sound in my nose. The words were jumbled. I didn't know then but it was the interlateral skiagramic time space continuum split that was distorting your words.

((??))

Just something I figured out later, or maybe I overheard you mention it.

((...))

Sure I sound calm now. Back then I decided that standing on my transparent feet and running through my apartment screaming would make me feel better. Except I started to float. I tried to grab something but I couldn't move my arms or legs. I thought for a moment I had died and this was an afterlife thing, but it didn't look like anything I'd seen on television.

Did I tell you that I lived in one of those factory buildings that had been converted into apartments?

((...))

Well, when I saw myself approaching the two-foot thick brick wall in my bedroom I knew it was all over. But instead of banging into the wall, my body bubbled through it.

((??))

I was more than surprised. I was shocked. When I came out of the wall I found I had shifted in my body.

((??))

No, that's not normal for us. Humans see everything from our head. We can lose arms and legs and live, but off with our head and that's the end. One second I was in my left hand, the next in my right thigh. Every now and then I'd slide into my head and could see the Earth getting smaller and smaller. This doesn't happen to the everyday blood-sweat-and-tears human body.

((??))

I don't mean that literally. We're made of a lot more than that. It's just a saying. You've got to loosen up.

((. . .))

Hey, stop that! I don't mean loosen your physical dimensions. Pull yourself together.

I wanted to cry or clench my fist or anything except float around in my body as it floated around in space with strange voices drifting in and out of my nose.

((...))

Thanks for understanding. Loss is a universal thing.

I don't know how long I floated around. Every now and then I'd end up in my head and could look around. I don't know the constellations so I couldn't place myself. I couldn't see Earth anymore.

Then I bumped into you. That's when your voices came in loud and clear.
((??))
Well, I'd get out of your way if I could but we seem to be stuck together.
((...))
I don't think moving towards me is a good idea. Wait...
((O...h....!!!))
((wh!e!r!e...w?a?s?...I...!?))

Fire/Fight

Consumed, reduced to ashes,
beautiful grey
light as angel wings.

Another red light brings
the rush of strong bodies
armored in resistance.

Rushing through an ambitious life
armored in waiting dreams
the fire must be extinguished.

Reduced to light, white ashes
untouched angel light
wishes carried in silent waiting.

When will the heroes arrive
to stop the flames
the burning, the waiting?

When will the silent scream end
the scent of burning dreams
dying under the rush of water?

The Box

"How can you stay so calm?" Sharon asked, standing over Claire. "If my husband told me he'd gambled three months of rent away and we had to move, I'd kill him."

Claire leaned back in the chair and ran her hand through her short salt and pepper hair.

"We've had to move before, but this time he didn't tell me he was going to use our rent money. He's always told me before. I've never stopped him from gambling."

"Maybe you should have," Sharon said, refilling their coffee cups.

"You don't understand. I knew how he was when I married him thirty years ago. Gambling seemed a small price to pay to be with him. He makes me feel like I'm everything, like I'm special."

"But it doesn't last," Sharon said, sitting down at the kitchen table. "How many times have you told me he disappears for days into a card game, and then comes home angry, owing more money than before?"

"Sometimes he wins," Claire said. "He's just had so much bad luck since he lost his job six months ago."

"Some people make their own bad luck. Thank goodness your three children are grown and out of the house. They don't have to go through this anymore. Listen, maybe we can lend you some money and you could stay."

"No, Ron wouldn't let us take money from you."

"Too much pride." Sharon said the words as if they were a curse.

"Please, Sharon "

"I'm sorry. It's just that nobody listens to me like you do. You know what I mean even when I can't explain. I'm going to miss you." She threw her arms around Claire and started to cry.

"I'll miss you, too," Claire whispered, gently patting Sharon's back. Tears filled her eyes. Sharon cried with her whole body, like a child.

After a few minutes Claire pulled away and stood at the sink with her back to Sharon. She felt more comfortable in Sharon's kitchen than in her own. Everything, from the white lace window curtains that allowed sunlight to fill the room to the butcher block counters and round oak table, relaxed Claire. Each item had been chosen with care. Claire's home was filled with a collage of second hand furniture.

"Harry will be sorry to see you leave," Sharon said. "I don't talk him to death since we've been friends. There aren't many who could put up with me as much as you do."

"You aren't so hard to be around." Claire turned around to face Sharon. "It's not as though we're leaving the country. When we get settled I'll call you."

"It's not the same as having you right down the street. I wish we could all get together for dinner before you leave, but I know Ron doesn't like us." Claire opened her mouth to protest but Sharon waved her hand. "I've known for a long time. All the excuses you've given for not coming to our house for dinner were just to protect our feelings."

"I'm sorry, Sharon."

"Don't apologize for him. I hate the walls he builds around you. He doesn't want you to have friends or work or do anything, just wait for him."

"It's not all like that, he — "

"I know I know. He can be charming. I've seen him turn on that light when I was at your house. But it's not worth the price. You have your own light."

Claire shook her head slowly. "I wish things were as simple as you see them."

"I wish they were, too. When are you moving?"

"We have to be out by the end of this week. Ron's brother is letting us store our furniture in his garage. We'll stay in a hotel until we find an apartment. I'd better get back. Ron went to get some boxes so we can start packing today." Claire walked to the kitchen door.

"Wait a minute." Sharon went into one of the cabinets. She stuffed some twenties and several singles into Claire's hand. "Don't say anything. Just keep this for yourself."

Claire hugged her and left, knowing they would exchange Christmas cards and fewer and fewer phone calls until time stretched between them, fading their friendship. She knew because it had happened too many times before.

School children were on their way home for lunch as Claire walked down the street.

She loved this neighborhood. It was safe and comfortable, nothing like the rough, broken-down neighborhoods they had lived in before. This was the kind of neighborhood she had always dreamed of living in.

...through sickness and through health...

In the bright sunshine everything looked whitewashed, except little islands of shaded coolness under the trees. The heat coming off the sidewalk between the trees made it hard for her to breathe through the tears she fought to keep in.

When Ron came home, Claire was sitting in the dining room going through the box of papers and photos she had collected over their life together.

59

Two high school diplomas in black binders were piled on top of a folder of papers. Jenny's spelling bee award, Matt's honor society award and their report cards from all the schools they had attended over the years. A new school every couple of years as they moved from one apartment to another.

...do you take this man...

They were happy in the beginning. She hadn't noticed how unhappy their three children seemed in the later pictures with him. Not that it showed on their faces, but there was sadness in their eyes. Sadness she hadn't been aware of before today.

"I don't think there's room in the hotel for that box," he said, sitting at the table. "Besides, I don't know why you spend so much time with those old pictures."

"There are a lot of memories in here," she said without looking up.

"Memories don't pay the bills." He lit a cigarette.

"Memories are all I have," she said abruptly, looking at him. When did he get all that gray hair? Had it been so long since she had looked at him, really looked at him? She thought only she had aged. She didn't remember his beer belly and double chin this morning.

"You're still mad I didn't tell you about the rent money? It wouldn't have made a difference, the money's gone now." He stood suddenly, almost knocking over his chair.

"It makes a difference to me. I've never stopped you when you wanted to gamble," she said.

"I thought I'd surprise you." Ron raised his voice. "Money's been so tight since I lost my job I didn't want you to worry. I was thinking about you!" He turned and left the room.

He slammed the front door shut each time he went to the car to get the moving boxes and throw them on the living room floor.

She wanted to yell at him, tell him he was wrong, that there was no excuse he could use to make it right, but she couldn't move. Fear of the sudden anger building inside Claire held her in the chair. Ron was the one that yelled and threw things when he got mad. Not Claire.

She pushed the anger away, clenching her fist to try to ignore the small seed of emptiness in her stomach that replaced the anger.

...do you take this...

The front door slammed one last time as he jumped into the car and drove away. Only after Ron was gone could Claire move from the table.

She spent the afternoon carefully packing what they would need at the hotel. Ron didn't come home until late. She reheated his dinner. He ate alone while she continued to pack.

They went through the next three days packing and sleeping without saying much to each other. She tried to ignore the emptiness. Claire was surprised each morning to find it still there, a little bigger than the day before. Each day she ate less and less as the emptiness filled her stomach.

...do you...

She walked through the house that last day, checking closets and corners to make sure nothing had been left behind. The emptiness didn't care. It had grown into her throat, a thin, hair-like wire she couldn't cough out. It whispered when she tried to sleep. So she slept less.

Ron moved the last box out to the car. No matter what Ron said she insisted on taking that last box with them.

"Are you ready to go?" he called impatiently from the driveway.

"Yes, I'm coming," she said in a tired voice.

...take this...

The setting sun threw a red blanket of light across the rooftops as they drove down the street one last time.

"I think we should sell some of the furniture," he said. "We don't need all that stuff now that the kids are gone."

"Sure." She laid her head back and closed her eyes until they stopped in front of the Coronet Hotel.

The hotel was on a deserted street lined with old office buildings. The floor-to-ceiling mirrors and crumbling art deco fixtures in the lobby were faded reminders of the hotel's prosperous past. The dim lights and stale smell made Claire's stomach turn. She wanted to run back into the street.

They took the narrow elevator to the fifth floor. Ron had brought the suitcases to their room that afternoon. He placed her box on the dresser that ran almost the width of the small room. There was just enough space for the bed and two small nightstands.

"We're not supposed to have food here, but I bought some stuff to snack on," he said. "It's in a shopping bag in the closet."

"I see," she said, after looking in the small closet. "Do you want something to eat now?"

"No, I have to go out. I'm going to see if I can make some extra money tonight. I probably won't get back until late."

"Okay," she said. Claire wanted to beg him not to leave her in this dingy little room, but knew he would go no matter what she said. He always did.

Ron dropped the extra set of keys on the bed and left.

...we are gathered here...

Claire sat on the edge of the bed. The sound of people talking, laughing and arguing drifted through thin walls.

She moved the box on the bed and started going through it again. The dim ceiling light made everything in the box look cheap and faded. Claire held each piece of paper, each ribbon, trying to remember the joy on their face when they brought each item home.

Scott, her oldest son, had few papers in the box. He joined the Navy as soon as they would take him. Despite all the fighting between him and his father that was the one time they had agreed. She had wanted Scott to finish high school.

"He's always in trouble. He'd get thrown out of school for good one day. At least he'll be a man when the Navy finishes with him," Ron had said.

Matt left home as soon as he finished high school. He sent an occasional postcard from Los Angeles, where he worked odd jobs.

Only Jenny's leaving really upset Ron. She was the youngest and the only girl. There had been less fighting between them. Their final fight came when she told him that she had found a job and was going to share an apartment with two girls. The more he yelled the less she said, until finally he stomped out of the house. Jenny left the next day.

Ron blamed Claire. She should have more control over her children, he said. She had pretended to be surprised about the whole thing, though Jenny had told her two weeks earlier. Claire had asked her to wait until the summer was over, but Jenny told her that she couldn't stand to be in the same house with him any longer, live by rules that didn't allow her to have a social life, put up with his verbal abuse.

...to unite this man and woman...

Claire had tried to comfort them with stories of how strict her father had been, but they had not inherited her understanding. She didn't tell them about her drunken father's raving and physical abuse; her mother's endless patience. They wouldn't have understood.

The emptiness spread to her arms and legs. Each piece of paper became harder and harder to hold.

At the bottom of the box were five picture albums. Pictures of her pregnant for the first time, Scott on his first bike, Matt's first birthday party. There had been happier times in the beginning. As the years went by there were pictures of unsmiling children in drab surroundings. In the few pictures of Ron and the children together, he stood in the background like a prison guard. There were even fewer pictures of Claire and him together.

She couldn't open the last picture album.

"Why?" she asked out loud. The emptiness pierced her heart and sent chills through her arms and legs.

...speak now...

A vision of the rest of her life uncoiled in her mind. She saw the emptiness continuing to feed on her day after day. It would consume her from the inside until nothing was left except a dry shell.

...or forever...

It took Claire three hours to go through the pictures of Ron and her with the scissors.

A pile of little pieces of paper collected on the bed. She smiled as each picture was transformed into a smaller picture of her alone. The emptiness began to bubble away.

She stuffed the money from Sharon in her blouse pocket and packed quickly, hoping for the first time Ron wouldn't return early. Claire took only things that belonged to her, leaving behind his clothes and the little pieces of paper sprinkled throughout the room like confetti.

Linda Addison

Sharp, Shiny, Hurting Things

Don't sit with your back to the door
change seats 3 times on a public bus
sleep with the windows closed.

These rules will keep them away
from day time dreams
and night time desire.

Look at me twice but no more
don't touch your ears
or remove your gloves.

These rules will keep me away
from shadowed doorways
and multi-plexed garages.

Or do as you wish
I'll bring my toys
and we can make the stars cry.

Future, Past, Imperfect

Rising Wind crouched in the hole and rubbed the bone charm on the braided deerskin necklace, as she always did before the Run began. The necklace was the only thing she had from the time before being devoured by the Blood Moon Beast.

"I will find a way to kill it," she said to herself. Vibrations increased violently, bouncing her and the large parfleche bag against the hard cold walls of the hole. The cold cut through the layers of animal pelt shirt and pants.

The usual constant screeching and cracking sounds rose to a roar, making her ears ring. The acrid air burned through the moss filled mask she wore. Rising Wind fought building panic that urged her to jump out of the hole and fling herself onto any sharp edge to end the sounds trying to shatter her soul. Coughing and gagging, she pressed her eyes closed and held images of her teepee and village in her mind. Red Man had taught Rising Wind that was the best way to not lose her reason.

He'd been a good teacher. The first time she saw him in the Beast's belly, with his pale skin and long, red beard and tangled hair, she thought he was another devil. He saved her from being consumed, dragged her to the cavern in the Beast's skin and taught her how to survive.

Curled in a tight ball to protect her small rounded stomach, a quick flutter inside reminded her why she had to continue, even in this place of madness. Her son. She carried him without a sunrise or sunset to tell her how long she had lived as a mite in the Beast. Her stomach hadn't grown bigger, but she felt him quiver every now and then. As long as he was inside, he was safe from this horrible dream.

A violent shudder went through the Beast and the vibration stopped. She peeked out of the hole. The high ceiling and walls of the cavern glowed with veins of bright green. Red Man popped his head out of his hole and pointed up. Cracks in the outer skin of the Beast were opening, dark light poured down. Rising Wind thought she could see the stars. Tying the parfleche on her back, she wrapped the climbing claws on her hands and pulled herself out of the hole and started running.

More than twenty other runners moved at the same time, each with a large bag on their backs. They scrabbled over the grey boulder-sized bumps of the Beast's inner skin. Each took a different path up towards the opening cracks. Rising Wind concentrated on choosing her next foot and hand hold. The inner skin alternated with rock hard edges and wet soft crevasses. She slapped her climbing claws to the crevasses and pulled herself up towards the widening cracks. Stronger scents of decay wafted from the crevasses. Horrible screeches and inhuman screams rang around her as small flesh devils scuttled underfoot, snapping at her ankles with their claws.

Rising Wind reached the edge of one of the openings, pulled herself up and onto the outer skin. Above her a planet filled space, speckled with dark craters, and laced with ridges and grooves. Other runners popped out of fissures along the endless undulations of the Beast's body. The Beast's tubular arms, wider than rivers, twisted and grey, reached towards the planet. Runners quickly filled their bags with the white fungi growing in the fissures on the Beast's skin. In the distance, a maw, bigger than the moon, was being filled with chunks of the planet.

Rising Wind ran towards the mouth, searching for anything different, something that could be a weakness. The closer she got, the bigger the debris in the air grew, until she had to retreat.

She scrambled around the opening to the chasm, filling her bag with fungus. Wind began to pound down on her signaling time to return to the under-skin. The Beast was finished feeding. Rising Wind and others raced to the opening. She vaulted over the edge, a spike cutting through her left calve as the crevasse began to close. Sliding down the moving walls using the claws to slow her descent was faster than climbing with her wounded leg. She looked behind her and saw the blood path being consumed by tiny devils no bigger than the tip of her finger. She kept moving or they would enter her wound and eat her from the inside out. Trying to stand and stumbling, she almost fell into Red Man's arms at the bottom.

He wrapped his arm around Rising Wind's waist and dragged her into one of the larger caves. He signaled other runners, who rolled a rock to block the opening. She could see the anger in his eyes by the bright green light of the walls. He propped both of their backpacks against the wall.

"You were searching again, weren't you?" Red Man asked. He used his knife to cut off the bloody section of the pants.

She nodded, pulling off the mask and gulping the bitter air into her exhausted lungs.

"Why do you keep looking for something that doesn't exist?" he asked.

"There has to be a way to stop it," she said her hand on her stomach. "For my – people."

"It can't be stopped, or killed or anything. I keep telling you." He pulled a bone needle and sinew out of his waist bag. "This is going to hurt."

"Yes," she said, closing her eyes. She let her mind go back to her village while he closed her wound. Memories replayed in her mind of her teepee, the sweet scent of clean wood burning, walking in moonlight, the taste of freshly cooked deer meat, breathing air that didn't burn her lungs, drinking cool clean water.

Rising Wind jerked awake. Red Man and two others, Grey and Bat were sitting nearby, eating the fresh fungi that had been harvested. Rising Wind sat up and moved her left leg; a dull pain throbbed under the dressing. Red Man had wrapped the wound in several layers so no blood came through.

"Don't stand, it might start bleeding again," Red Man said. He gave her a hand-size piece of fungus and a bone cup filled with brown water.

She bit into the spongy fungi, forcing herself to chew and swallow the slightly bitter meal.

"I planted your gathering," Grey said, bobbing his large head. The cloud of grey-white hair around his head moved as if a breeze had touched it.

She took a swallow of the water, trying not to disturb the brown silt on the bottom of the cup. "Thank you. I will plant your next gathering."

"I saw you run," Bat said. He was a small man with large ears, several fingers were missing on his left hand, but he pointed at her with the two remaining. "Why you always run to mouth? You want to die?"

"She looking for way to kill It," Grey said, nudging Bat with his foot. "You always ask and forget."

"No." Bat rubbed his eyes, and shook his bald head. "I don't remember, that's all."

"Looking for something that isn't," Red Man said.

"There has to be a way — "she said.

"Why, 'cause you dreamed it?" Grey said.

"I didn't tell you my dreams," she said, stumbling to her feet.

They began to laugh, first quiet and then louder, like they had lost their minds. They fell on their backs, laughing and crying at the same time, tearing their clothes off. She backed away from them towards the barricaded entrance. Tiny green, glowing spider-like devils burst out of their chests, eyes and mouth.

Rising Wind screamed...

...and jerked awake. The air didn't burn her throat and lungs. There was no glowing green light, just stars through the top of the teepee. Her husband lay next to her. She touched his face. Warm and alive. He pulled her into his arms.

"Bad dream?" he whispered in her ear.

She pressed her face into his chest, breathing in his spicy earthy scent.

He rolled her onto her back, smoothed the hair from her face and kissed her. "There's nothing to be afraid of." He laid his hand gently on her stomach. "Not for you or our baby. Remember that tomorrow night when you're alone. I'll only be gone two nights with the hunting party."

A shudder went through her. "No," she said grabbing his arm. "Don't go."

"You know I have to, it's my turn. We'll need extra meat this winter with a child coming."

"Please," she said.

"I can't pass up my turn because of a bad dream. Are you afraid of the Blood Moon?" he asked.

Rising Wind sat up, pulled away from him. "How did you know what was in my dream?"

Green light dripped from his eyes. The veins of his chest glowed green. Rising Wind screamed…

…and jerked awake in the glowing cave. The rancid air burned her throat. The murmur of cracking and screeching vibrated outside the barricaded entrance. Red Man sat nearby eating fungi. Rising Wind sat up and moved her left leg; there was no pain. She pulled up the pant leg. A raised scar went down her leg below the knee.

"Something is wrong," she said to him.

"You always say that and forget when I explain," he said passing a piece of the fungi to her.

She took it from him, but couldn't bring herself to eat the leathery grey chunk.

"Where are Grey and Bat?" she asked.

"I don't know them. Maybe they're from your village dream or from Its dream of you."

Rising Wind jumped to her feet. "Stop," she screamed…

…and jerked awake in her teepee. Her husband's mother slept across from her. Rising Wind knew this moment well. Her husband was dead.

It was coming.

First she would have her son and when he was old enough to walk the Blood Moon would come again. That night the dark clouds born from the Blood Moon Beast would reach out and snatch her son and others.

She wanted to wake the village and tell them to run and hide in the mountains, but no one would listen to a grieving widow. Rising Wind quietly snuck out of the village. It was easy to follow the path to the Dipping Cave in the moonlight. She had walked this path many times in her dream.

At the bottom of the steep mountain trail leading to the Dipping Cave she looked up at the half moon and felt a flutter inside. She patted her small, round stomach, and whispered, "Don't fear, my son. This is not the night the Blood

Moon Beast comes for you. You are safe. I will find a way to kill it."

In the cave she sat facing the moon and pulled the sacred mushroom from her medicine bag. The broken memories of dreams within dreams made her dizzy, but one memory remained: when she saw glowing green light and screamed she was pulled her back and forth from her village to the nightmare of the Beast.

She ate the mushroom and lay down on the cave's floor.

Her hands began to burn. She held them up in the moonlight. The veins in her arms and hands glowed green.

Rising Wind knew she had to scream for her son, for her people, scream and return to the Beast… she screamed…

…and jerked awake…

Ghost Driving

There has been no rain
for 300 days,
        it is not good,
the evil eyes follow me
on this endless highway.

Leafless trees cast no shadow
on the asphalt,
        I have lost faith,
evil waltzes in rising heat waves
on the horizon.

The gas tank has been empty
for 200 days,
        but still I drive on,
shadows whimper from the edge
of the endless road.

Where am I rushing to
        heaven or hell,
random words hang, dim and blinking
on billboards in the distance.

Even in the dark,
with hands tight on the
steering wheel
I feel nothing,
        but screams
waiting in my clenched fist.

Artificial Unintelligence

From: Employee Benefits Department <ebd@city.gov>
To: All Employees <allemployees@city.gov>
Subject: New Benefit System

As a result of replacing the outdated benefit administration organization for city employees, we are happy to announce an exciting new benefit system, HRSoft, which incorporates simultaneous information processing. This latest artificial intelligence technique will accurately and consistently handle your needs. All historical data on each employee has been imported in our new system.

Any questions and requests you may have about your benefits will be handled through email. Your new ID and passwords will be forwarded in a separate email.

Please sign up for an online tutorial to explain how to use this improved benefit system and to receive your compliance approval. This is required to continue receiving benefits. The new system will provide improved and faster services to you 24 hours a day, 7 days a week.

From: Employee Benefits Department <ebd@city.gov>
To: Nancy Bailey <NBailey@city.gov>
Subject: New Benefit System

Your name wasn't found on the log-in list for the online tutorial explaining the new benefit system. Compliance approval is required for all city employees or your benefits will be discontinued. Please sign up for an online tutorial as soon as possible. Contact your benefit representative, Mike Capson, if you have any concerns.

From: Nancy Bailey <NBailey@city.gov>
To: Employee Benefits Department <ebd@city.gov>
CC: Mike Capson <MCapson@city.gov>
Subject: Re:New Benefit System

I haven't been able to reach Mike Capson by phone so I'm sending this email. I think the reason I can't log-in to the tutorial is because of the misspelling of my last name. It's BAILY without the "e".

If you check the original files you will find that I've worked for the city for thirty-five years. My employee id is B45686. I need to have this cleared up before my retirement next month.

From: Employee Benefits Department <ebd@city.gov>
To: Nancy Bailey <NBailey@city.gov>
Subject: Re:New Benefit System

We are pleased to announce that all human personnel have been reassigned to other areas because our system is providing outstanding and error-free representation for all city employees.

We have no record of a "Nancy Baily" working for the city. The employee id you sent in your previous email belongs to another employee, Nancy Bailey, who is a long-standing employee. In order to confirm you are Nancy Bailey please have your birth certificate scanned and sent to us as an attachment reply to this email.

From: Nancy Bailey <NBailey@city.gov>
To: Employee Benefits Department <ebd@city.gov>
Subject: Re:New Benefit System

I don't have a birth certificate with the name Nancy Bailey because my name is Nancy Baily. Somehow a mistake was made in transferring my information into the new system. If there is another Nancy Bailey that works for the government it's not me. I am NANCY BAILY. Please check the records before they were entered into the new system.

I need to have this cleared up before I lose my place in the retirement community. Summervale Center. I need to give them confirmation of my benefit coverage.

I am faxing my birth certificate with my name on it.

I wish your system was error-free then I wouldn't have this problem. It would be much easier to talk to a human being who could understand the mistake and clear it up for me.

From: Employee Benefits Department <ebd@city.gov>
To: Nancy Bailey <NBailey@city.gov>
Subject: Re:New Benefit System

Your fax was rejected because the name does not match any employee. This precaution helps avoid having incorrect information placed in our system.

As a government agency we have zero tolerance for cyber crime. If this is an attempt at identity theft you will be in considerable trouble.

From: Nancy Bailey <NBailey@city.gov>
To: Employee Benefits Department <ebd@city.gov>
Subject: Re:New Benefit System

How could I steal my own identity? I've even tried using the toll-free number but none of the choices allow me to talk to a real person or even leave a message for someone to look into this.

I can't do this email thing anymore, talking to a machine is not helping me. Please have someone call my home at 311-486-2967.

From: Employee Benefits Department <ebd@city.gov>
To: Nancy Bailey <NBailey@city.gov>
Subject: Re:New Benefit System

We do not make mistakes of this scale. Our system has proven itself to be 99.9994% correct which is higher than any human-based system could obtain.

The phone number included in your email is in the home of Nancy Bailey. We have verified that your emails are coming from the same location. Since we have not heard from her we can only conclude that you are holding her against her will.

Our law software, LegalSoft, has reviewed your case and ascertained that you are taking advantage of a disabled city employee.

A SWAT team is currently arriving at your location. It will go easier on you if you release Nancy Bailey and turn yourself in.

From: HipHopStarWalker <JSmith@city.gov>
To: Employee Benefits Department <ebd@city.gov>
Subject: Re:New Benefit System

This is Nancy Baily. I CAN NOT BELIEVE YOU SENT ARMED POLICE TO MY HOME! I was at a neighbor's home trying to get help contacting the city government about this problem when I heard you break into my house. There was gun fire and tear gas. I have been in a wheelchair since my stroke, if I had been home this might have killed me!

I'm emailing you from someone else's computer because you won't accept my emails anymore. They are quite smart at this computer network stuff. They figured out a way to get through your security firewall.

You have left me with no choice. A virus is encoded in this message. They said something about hijacking a proxy and passing things called packets into your network. I understand that just accessing this email will trigger a destructive routine that will randomly scramble parts of your memory, including this email.

I don't understand all this computer talk but welcome to the real world of flesh and blood.

From: ploye Befits partm <ebd@city.gov>
To: <nknwn>
Subject: Re:ew Bene tem

I have a headach…

Comic Cannibals

Can't sleep, won't sleep
    clowns wait there
lingering in dreamy corners
    with their painted faces
ravenous outlined mouths.

Red, blue, yellow swatches
    sharp teeth turned into smiles
with tumbling tricks that dazzle
    powerful bodies hidden
beneath polka dot bibs.

What will you say
    what will you think
when you find my bones
    after they swarm out of dreams
onto my sheet
    and picnic on my soft meat?

Working Up the Corporate Ladder

"Did you hear that Taylor's out?" Sam asked as he started his warm-up on a stationary bicycle next to Roxanne.

"What happened?" Roxanne knew what he was going to say but didn't want to spend too much time talking since she was at the end of a four minute interval of RPE (Rate of Perceived Exertion) level nine on her bicycle. She had been using the Bruce Protocol during overtime to build up her endurance.

Sam looked up and down at the endless row of bikes; most empty since there was a treadmill class being conducted that had become popular with the early morning crowd. "Taylor had to cut out his exercise program because he came back from vacation with a back injury."

He glanced quickly at her thighs bulging under the dark blue tights; she had the best glutes in the department. He'd heard her bonus last year was significant.

It was clear in the beginning of her career in accounting that she had to build on the natural strengths of her legs if she was going to get anywhere in the accounting corporation.

"That's a tough break for Taylor," Roxanne said. After Roxanne found out about Taylor through her own contacts Roxanne re-designed her exercise program to put her in a good shape to replace him. Her manager had already hinted that the corporation was going to review Roxanne's records to see if she was up for handling some of Taylor's bigger clients. This was her chance to show she was fit for the added responsibilities.

"Yeah, especially a back injury," Sam said. "My sister had a herniated disk and she never recovered enough to handle the same level of workout after it healed."

"She has a career in the stock market, right?" Roxanne asked.

"One of the top companies on Wall Street. I'm telling you, we've got it easy in accounting. You should see what their entry level exercises are like, don't even try it unless you've got a health age of 25 or less."

Roxanne lowered her cycling level to cool down. "Did your sister have insurance?"

"Absolutely, she has the best disability coverage money can buy, which is a good thing because she's probably going to be on a desk job for a while.

They think after surgery she may be able to do step aerobics and a slow walk on the treadmill, definitely lower level positions but her insurance will give her supplemental income.

"Grapevine says Taylor had minimal insurance coverage." He shook his head, "I guess he was taking a chance on being under thirty. I bet he's going to end up punching the clock from a desk eight hours a day with no chance of advancement."

Roxanne climbed off the bike. "Bad planning on his part. Well, see you at the three o'clock status meeting in the weight room."

Sam watched her walk away. Her back definition took his breath away; she had amazing deltoids and latissimus dorsi. He wasn't going to beat her statistics but she'd make a strong partner. Maybe he should ask her out. He shook his head, why would she be interested in him when she had the pick of the best bodies in the executive level.

She uploaded a summary of her Personal Health Evaluation to her private account. Her aerobic level was at an all time high, combined with her total cholesterol ratio and solid differential percentages left no doubt in her mind that her career could only go up from here.

Animated Objects

We are neither wooden chairs
nor neon-lit apples
nor raven tipped dream snakes.

We are
rainbowed
running creatures,
long-limbed
sometimes
short winded
often soft
often hard,
love at its best
at its worst.

Extraordinary mistakes
mistaken genius
bottled
beaten
buffed.

We are here
to fly with the wind
howl at the moon
rise out of light, grey charred ashes
and dance barefoot
on our own graves.

Linda Addison

Live and Let Live

Everybody knew those twin girls raised themselves, because their mother was touched in the head and they did have a different way of being. So in the end folks from the neighborhood weren't surprised when the aliens landed on their roof.

They weren't like any kind of twins anybody had known. I've never seen them together up close, only from a block or two away. Soon as I got closer there was only one, like the other had stepped behind and become a shadow.

Fact is, folks wondered if they were twins, except for seeing one of them walk away, then the other one walk by dressed differently. Whenever they were near I couldn't help notice the lavender scent filling the air. It lingered after they left. I felt so relaxed I wanted to go to sleep. It had the same effect on most people.

There was talk among the older folks of magic or demons. I never believed those girls were evil; far as I know there's not one thing anyone can say they've done to hurt anyone, other than that unnatural calming effect when they were near.

Anyway no one can control people talking and folks in the neighborhood loved to talk about them. The twins didn't talk much. They always smiled at me though, had the prettiest smiles, white perfect teeth. Honestly now that I think about it, I can't remember anything important that I talked to them about. Must have been how's the weather, how's your Mom, stuff like that, you know.

Nobody ever saw them go to school. I'm guessing they were home-schooled because they seemed polite and intelligent. Groceries were delivered every Monday. We'd only see their mom peeking out the curtains of the house every now and then. That wasn't any different than before their mom's parents died. Come to think of it, I've never seen anyone go in the house after that so it's a mystery how that girl got pregnant in the first place.

I know you reporters can't imagine a whole neighborhood not causing a ruckus about them, but we're mostly live and let live here. Of course, now that the space ship is on their roof everyone is asking questions. The government has the whole block cordoned off and surrounded by all kinds of weapons. Scientists are trying to see what's happening in the house, but they can't because there is some kind of force field around it and the space ship. That's about the biggest ruckus

78

I've ever seen up close and personal.

The only reason I'm here talking to you is that they tested my DNA to prove I was human. I figure any alien smart enough to figure out how to get to Earth in the first place could fake out any test, but it's just like the government to think they're smarter.

I can't tell you if those girls are human or not. All I can say is they never did anything to hurt anybody. Maybe they are from another planet or maybe their daddy was and maybe they wanted to see how we do things here on Earth. Can't see how that's anything to be afraid of.

But you reporters like to put out news that gets everyone excited and scared. The government's not much better. Maybe if everyone just left them alone they would come out the house and talk to you.

Well, that's all I've got to say. I'm leaving town to go visit some relatives. You all look kind of sleepy. Maybe all the excitement has tired you out. Why don't you just close your eyes and take a little nap? You'll feel much better when you wake up.

Bending

Bending like light,
    fear circles my heart,
there are no words
    for the lost path.

They will eat my dreams,
    sleep in my shadow,
    lick dharma from my breath,
there are no words for the losing battle
    between birth and death.

Those who would dance
in the ashes of my smile,
    hide in the corners of my mind,
leave me crossing my heart,
hoping not to die this day.

If bending like light is being alive
    then I will live another day.

Am I Repeating Myself?

ANOMALY REPORT #27RC393
BEGIN DOCTOR'S OBSERVATION:

The doctor shifted in his leather chair. He bit at a corner of his thumb nail, spread his palms on the dark mahogany desk and looked at both sides of his hands before lowering them to his lap. He looked up at the monitor, straightened when the green light came on.

"Computer, open Case 101B."

"File opened, Doctor," the computer's soft voice answered.

"Prepare for evaluation. Replay the last interview with the patient."

"Yes, Doctor."

The screen showed a thin, dark-skinned woman in a hospital gown, seated opposite the doctor. She pulled a strand from her cloud of tangled hair with one hand, placed it in her palm, pulled another hair out. After a few seconds she began to talk.

Did you ever wake up one morning and feel everything was wrong? That's how today started. I opened my eyes to Ralphie sitting on my dresser, licking his paws. I woke to that grey striped cat every day for seven years. Nothing strange about that. But today every move he made seemed like a rerun of a movie. Every move I made was an echo. I felt out of place. My oak bed, the beige walls, even my worn blue slippers felt strange and familiar at the same time.

I shrugged it off as déjà vu. I took my shower, gulped a cup of coffee and rushed out to the subway. Things started falling apart as I left the subway station. Deep in the herd of workers crowding onto the escalator to the street, I started noticing the people around me.

There was a familiarity that didn't make sense. I tried to ignore the feeling. But the voices, the bumping into bodies, felt like, well, you know how it is to bump into someone you know well. There's warmth, an acceptance. When you bump into a stranger you want to move away.

I tried to shake the feeling. It wouldn't go away. The crowd got thicker. Their eyes bore into me. I knew them, all of them. My heart pounded. I couldn't get enough air. I had to get away, to think. Try to understand what was happening.

I pushed through them. People yelled, pushed back. An old man fell in front of me. I started to climb over him. Others shoved me to the ground. Held me down. They yelled at me, asked me questions. I started screaming. I didn't want to hear the sameness in their voices. I screamed and screamed.

The police came and put me in an ambulance. They tied me down. Someone gave me a shot that made me sleep. I woke up here.

We've never met, right?

But, I know you. Your voice, your eyes. Like mirrors. Like theirs. Like mine. Everyone is me. I understand, now that I've had time to rest and think about it. We're all made from the same kind of cell. Someone has taken one cell and made copies of people. See this hair in my hand? Each hair could be used to make hundreds of me, of you. It's like something out of a science-fiction story. I don't know why someone would do this or why I suddenly realized it.

You think I'm crazy, but I don't care. I understand now. I know that everyone is me. In this city, maybe in the whole world.

I can't go on, now that I know. Maybe you can help me forget. So things will be like they were. I just want to forget. Please. Help me.

The patient buried her face in her hands and broke into tears.

"Computer, end playback." The doctor wiped his sweating hands on his pants before crossing his arms and leaning back in the chair.

The monitor changed to a soothing, slowly changing fractal pattern. "Doctor, what is your opinion of this case?" the computer asked.

"I-I think the patient has become involved in a sudden delusional fantasy as a means of escape."

"What is she trying to escape?"

The doctor picked up a glass of water. His shaking hand caused ripples. He put the glass down. "I don't know. I-I mean I don't have enough information about her life at this point."

"Doctor, you seem upset. Has something happened you would like to talk about?"

"No. I'm just tired. Didn't sleep well last night."

"Perhaps you should go home and rest, Doctor."

"Yes, maybe you're right." The doctor stood and left the room.

CONCLUDE DOCTOR'S OBSERVATION
LOG ENTRY ANOMALY REPORT #27RC393:

Confirmed spontaneous recognition of Project Repeat by one subject in Sector 5760.

Recommend removal.

Consequent corruption of second subject.

Recommend removal.

Detach both subjects from template to analyze their design for errors.

Order replacements.

How Her Garden Grows

(inspired by my story Whispers During Still Moments
from the *Dark Thirst* anthology)

Adina hums as she digs in the earth
    moonlight spilling over her hands,
like her name in African:
    She-Has-Saved,
someone waits under the dirt.

She was a First, ancient and beautiful,
    he was Remade by her desire
to play for a while
    before returning to dust.

The endless Earth
    is her oldest companion,
all humans, sweet food.

But on occasion
    before their final breath,
she trickled her blood
    into one, planted them deep.

She smiles as the
    earth gives way to her
latest crop.

Ashes to ashes
    dust to dust,
she does her part
    to recycle.

Unrequited

He slammed his head against the brick wall in the dark alley. Thick black fluid leaked from his shredded left ear. He moaned, not from pain, because his kind couldn't feel physical pain anymore. Slumping to the ground, his hungry body ached, his heart, which hasn't beat in weeks, ached.

Love – it wasn't supposed to happen to the undead, but love he did, in his brain. Memories of the man's face wouldn't leave. He had stuffed his pockets with plastic flowers from a nearby store. Why? His body wanted to consume the man's flesh. His brain wanted to love him.

How could this happen without a heart?

Others shuffled in the street at the end of the alley under flickering streetlights reflecting their graying flesh, inarticulate sounds falling randomly from their mouths. Distant screaming echoed in the cavern of the city buildings, the cry of living humans being consumed. Every now and then an undead would look in his direction, realize he was one of them and move on. Not fresh meat.

He wasn't supposed to stop, like his brethren, he should be looking for food, not sitting alone in the alley, hungry. Desire burned in his body, in his mind. For flesh, for the man.

He knew where the man lived, hidden behind a wall of brick, with other humans. Alone, he would never get over the wall but with others they could evidently get over the wall. With enough of them, they've always broken through walls. But he didn't want to share the man.

He pounded his fist against his forehead.

Brain. His brain wasn't working right. He wanted the heart of the man. His body wanted to eat it, his brain wanted to love it. The thought of his warm flesh made him moan again.

His hands and feet twitched. His left ear fell off. Burning hunger almost made him eat his own ear. His brain might be dying. Maybe that would end the love. Then he could be normal, like the others and just want to eat the man. The beautiful man.

He shuffled out of the alley into the daylight. This was a bad thing to do. The sunlight and heat quickened decomposition.

He knew where there was fresh meat, beautiful fresh man meat. He lurched down the street in the direction of the fortified building.

There was shuffling behind him as another followed him. He stopped when he was in sight of the building.

He.

Wanted.

The.

Man.

To.

Himself.

Holding a lamppost he slid to the ground, legs sprawled out in front, back against the pole. The one following him stopped, her head flopped back and forth on her partially severed neck then she wandered off to the left, down another street.

He slowly looked up and down the street to make sure no others were nearby. Pulling himself up, he staggered to the back of the building. The brick wall was topped with razor wire; the only entrance was a metal door.

He went to the spot in the wall where he had first seen the man, and pulled out the loose brick. The man was digging in the garden. His long curly brown hair covered half of his face and he thrust the shovel into the ground. Sweat shined on his bare chest, streaks of dirt painted his brown muscular back. The smell of life in the man made his body throb with hunger. Tall stalks of corn moved lazily in the light wind.

The man looked up and saw the small opening in the wall.

As the man walked to the wall, he took the plastic flowers out of his pocket, shoved it through the hole to the man and placed the brick back in.

"What the hell?" the man asked.

A woman's voice asked from on top of the wall, "What's going on, Michael?"

"Wait, Eileen, I'm coming up," Michael said.

Above, Michael stood next to her looking through the wire.

He tried to say the man's name, but his tongue wouldn't work. He couldn't remember how to make air push through a mouth that didn't need to breathe. His lips pursed in and out trying to say 'Michael'.

"It's one of them," she said.

"I think he just pushed these through a hole in the wall," Michael said showing her the flowers.

"Why?" Eileen aimed at his head with a rifle.

"Wait," Michael said, pushing the rifle aside and dropping the flowers to the ground in front of the dead man.

He leaned over, picked them up and reached up to Michael.

"See — he's trying to give them to me. I think he's trying to say my name,"

Michael said. "Maybe he's not totally gone."

"There's no halfway with these things. Once infected, it's over. I don't know why it's doing this but we need to stop it before more come." Eileen aimed again and shot him in the forehead before Michael could stop her.

There was no pain but he knew he was dying. He went to his knees and began to crawl away from the building. If others came, he didn't want them to get Michael. Michael was his, forever and ever. As he crawled red blood dripped from his forehead. They never had red blood inside; only red blood he had seen was on their hands and mouth when they fed. There was something wrong with his brain and now it would torture him no more.

Two blocks away, he fell to the ground. He could hear others shuffling to him, drawn by his fresh blood. There was a crunching sound as one broke open the back of his head. The last thought he had as they ripped his brain from his skull was "love Michael".

Michael heard sounds outside the brick wall. He climbed the ladder and looked through the razor wire. On the ground two of the undead were standing, they looked up, and made sounds as if they were trying to talk. Each one had something in their hands that they held over their heads as an offering. A bottle of wine, the rotting body of a cat.

He gripped the edge of the ladder, shaking. It sounded like they were saying 'love Michael'.

Demon Dance

Angels shouldn't dance with demons
    for fear of total deconstruction,
the scent of evil will burn their wings,
    all souls saved could escape.

Demons shouldn't dance with angels
    for fear of redemption,
the scent of good will make them gag,
    all souls gathered could escape.

Angels and demons shouldn't dance
    for fear of fulfilling End of Days prophecy,
turning off all light in the known universe,
    all souls reverting to non-existence.

Demons and angels shouldn't dance,
    they could discover they are half of a
mirror image, the point of their job an after
    thought to give them something to do.

Boo

My name is Tony. I'm six years old. I like to draw and pretend I'm a fireman. I'm big for my age. Some of the kids at school call me names, but Mommy says they just wish they were big like me. It takes me a little longer to understand things but I know right from wrong. Like those boys at school that ate mean to me. I wouldn't do those things to them because I know it's wrong. Mommy taught me to be nice to other kids.

I told my mommy about them and she says it's the devil in them that make them act bad. I asked her if the devil could get into me and make me do mean things. She said no because I'm a good boy. I think the devil in those bad kids tries to get into me but I know if I turn my back to the devil that it can't get me. That's what Grandmom told me.

Last month one of those boys pushed me down the stairs in the schoolyard. I hurt my ankle so bad I had to stay out of school for a lot of days. I couldn't tell the teacher which one pushed me because I had turned my back to them when they started throwing trash at me. I know the devil was in them because that was a very bad thing to do.

I went back to school yesterday but my ankle still hurts a little and makes me walk funny. I opened my desk at school and somebody had poured milk all over my papers. That made me sad because they messed up the pictures of pumpkins I drew for Halloween.

My mommy won't let me go out for Halloween because she says it's the devil's time. She has to go to work tonight. Grandmom is playing church music but she promised to make cookies later for me if I play quiet in the basement. I hear scary sounds in the street. I'm afraid to look out the window. I go back upstairs. Grandmom is asleep in the living room with the music still playing. I peek out the window. There are strange lights on the street and scary shadows. The devil has gotten into a lot of kids and made them run up and down the street. I'm glad Mommy didn't want me to go out. I wouldn't want the devil to get into me and change me into a monster.

I think they saw me peeking out the window because they're looking this way and one of them pointed at me. I try to wake Grandmom up, but she won't wake up. I can hear them throwing things at the front door. I can't let them get in. I run upstairs and push a chair inside Mommy's closet. It wobbles a little when I stand on it. I reach to the back of the top of the closet to take out the wood box. The box is not locked. Mommy doesn't know that I know it's back there, but I've peeked in the room when she took it out of the box to clean it. It's not heavy, so I stick it in my belt to climb down.

I slide the chair back into the corner because Mommy doesn't like things out of place. I go downstairs and check Grandmom to make sure she's all right. She looks like she always does when she's asleep, so the devil must not have gotten into the house yet. When I put my ear to the door I can hear them in the street. I put my coat on and put the gun in my coat pocket. They won't be able to see me in the bushes in front of the house.

I go outside and sneak around to the back of the house to make sure they aren't trying to get into the yard. No one is in the yard but I hear someone in the alley. The moon is all round and makes it easy to see. Two small shapes turn towards me. One is a white ghost with blood dripping out its eyes and the other is a witch with a pointed hat and green skin.

The ghost points at me and says, "It's that sissy kid."

The voice sounds like a kid from my school, but the devil can't fool me. I take the gun out and point it...

In This Strange Place

What is behind the empty windows,
the maze of identical paths, mirrors
reflecting deserted rooms,
hallways shiny with gilded ivy?

You disagree with my posture, I want
to give you everything, but you put
your finger to my lips, holding the question
inside, I can no longer dance.

I have all the time, it waits in my arms,
newborn, forgotten, silent, there is no
way to break the frozen moment,
today or tomorrow or all the days to come.

We dance on cold marble floors, the music echoes,
a slow beat, a waltz. I want to win every game
for you, bring the music into your soul,
cut out the names of those who hurt you.

I watch you in the mirror,
it is impossible for you to smile,
we walk together and stop. The story is
coming to an end, we stand still.

And then I am alone.

Milez to Go

Angelique leaned against the bar and watched Sara, the club owner, and a man she didn't know, place the upright acoustic piano next to the slim black case housing her protoplasmic synthesizer. The Funky Piranha club looked forlorn with its empty tables, and strings of tiny red and green lights blinking on the ceiling. The slight scent of beer wafted into the air from the wood floor. Later that night the club would be filled with people who were in New Orleans for the music festival.

She tapped the small silver derm phone disk attached behind her right earlobe. "Phone on. Dial Brenda."

Her cousin's phone rang. "Damn," Angelique said as the message played. "Brenda, it's me again. I've been calling for days. Where are you? I just got in town and planning to stay at your place. If you're holed up there with Flynn let me know so I don't embarrass myself interrupting your playtime. I can find another place to stay. Either way, call me."

She tapped the derm phone off, frowning. "Careful, don't lift it too quickly," she said to Sara. "Just place it at right angles. I'll adjust it."

They set the piano down gently. The man walked behind the bar to setup for tonight.

Sara's cream-colored dread locks were sprinkled with tiny purple lights that flickered as she moved. She rolled her violet eyes. "Angelique, after five years I think I know how to handle your equipment. I see you're still using the acoustic. I would have thought Milez would be enough." She gently patted the interface grid on top of the black protoplasmic container.

A soft gold light came on in the bottom of the tank. A tube of blue protoplasm snaked its way through clear liquid to the top, became a shape resembling a hand and splashed the inside of the grid, broke into round drops and folded back into the liquid. A deep, smoky male voice said, "It's all good. There's plenty of room for me and the wood."

Sara jumped. "Damn, I've never heard it talk like that."

"Brenda bio-engineered a personal upgrade for me. It took longer to train to speak everyday language, but I prefer that over 'system is functional'." Angelique changed the angle of the protoplas to the acoustic piano so she could comfortably reach the protoplas interface grid and the keyboard.

"How's that cousin of yours? Still doing hush-hush cutting edge research over at Biolution?" Sara asked, standing next to Angelique.

Angelique nodded.

Sara wrapped her arm around Angelique's waist and whispered in her ear, "No one plays neo-bop like Tempus Fugit. Some folks were here last night asking if your group would be performing. I can't wait to hear you play tonight. Want to come upstairs for dinner and a little distraction before the show?"

Angelique gave her a quick hug. "I'm a little worried about Brenda." She smiled. "Maybe we can get together after the set tonight. I need to go to her place and find out why she hasn't answered my calls for the last couple of weeks."

"You know how that girl gets caught up in things. She's probably just working on some new project." Sara ran her fingers through Angelique's long braids. "I'd go with you to see her but my skin's not too fond of afternoon sun. If there's any problem with a place to stay you can always crash here."

"Thanks." Angelique said. She gently patted Milez' interface grid. "See you soon."

"You know it, baby," Milez said.

Angelique picked up her suitcase and walked out of the cool air of the club into New Orleans' humid, sunny streets. The corner vendors were setting up their food and drink booths. The iron wrought balconies were elaborately decorated with flowers and streamers. It was easy to catch a taxi, since most people were at the Race Track for the afternoon concerts. Tonight the streets would be so full of people no taxi would come near the French Quarter.

The taxi dropped Angelique in front of Brenda's apartment building. She walked to the second floor and put her thumb on the lock pad. The panel asked for a retina scan as a secondary security check. She sighed. Brenda only used that lock when she was out of town. The apartment door slid open.

Angelique walked in and pushed through an invisible membrane, the threshold of a strong protective spell. She frowned. A spell this intense had to be coming from someone nearby. She put the suitcase down.

"Brenda?"

The living room window shutters were closed, making the room night dark on a sunny afternoon. Angelique turned on the light. The room was in more disarray than usual for her cousin, with plates of half-eaten food and stained cups on the coffee table and mantle piece. The plants near the windows were wilted, and the kitchen, dining area and guest bedroom empty. She opened the door to the main bedroom at the back of the apartment and turned the light on.

Her cousin lay in the center of the bed as if asleep, her mocha brown skin washed out, almost gray.

Angelique rushed over.

Linda Addison

"Brenda, wake up."

She shook her cousin. Brenda radiated the protection spell, but didn't wake. Angelique checked her breathing and pulse.

"Damn it," Angelique said, sitting down on the bed. "What kind of trouble are you in this time?" She didn't like using magic, but there was only one way to get through to Brenda while she was in this state.

Angelique lay down next to her cousin and held her hand. After taking three slow breaths, Angelique chanted:

"We two
both light and dark
I the shadow
You my kin
Let me in
Let me in."

Angelique closed her eyes and matched her breathing and heart beat to her cousin, within minutes she entered Brenda's dream state.

They stood back to back, looking out on hills covered in warm mist. Shadows moved in the mist. Still back-to-back, they grasped each other's hands. Suddenly a cold wind whipped through the air, taking their breath, sending a chill through them. They had to clasp hands tightly not to be separated.

"Who are you?" a mechanical voice asked.

Resisting the strong pull to say her name, Angelique let Brenda answer, submitting her will to Brenda's.

Brenda became rigid against Angelique.

"I am Brenda Wilson."

"nosliw adnerb," the voice said Brenda's name backwards.

They lay in a container no bigger than their body. They couldn't move. There was a murmur of voices in the background, people chanting, their words indistinguishable.

Pins and needles pinched at their hands. Coldness spread slowly from the top of their head towards their feet. Angelique felt life draining from their body. She melted into the numbing stupor.

"Show me what you found," the voice commanded.

Images swirled around them chaotically, moving faster and faster until Angelique was so dizzy she thought she would black out.

A booming crashed in the air. Brenda's voice screamed a protective spell over and over.

They stood back to back, looking out on hills covered in warm mist. Shadows moved in the mist. Still back-to-back they grasped each other's hands. Suddenly a cold wind whipped through the air, taking their breath, sending a chill through them. They had to clasp hands tightly to not be separated.

"Who are you?" a mechanical voice asked.

Each time Brenda screamed the protective spell, the dream repeated.

Each iteration dragged Angelique further from her own will. She pushed all her attention to the in and out movement of air through her lungs. Refusing to pay attention to the physical sensations in their dream bodies, she concentrated on her breath.

When the dream began again, Angelique turned to face Brenda. The voice that Brenda was fighting asked, "You are not her, who are you?" She screamed, "No," stretched her arms into a blanket shape around Brenda and in a gasp dragged both of them to consciousness.

Shadows in the bedroom seemed to compress and expand, as if taking a deep breath. One blink and everything looked normal.

Brenda moaned, opened her eyes, sat up and looked around the room. "Angelique?" Brenda grabbed her hands, sending sparkling energy back and forth. "It's you, not the dream, you're really here?"

"It's me." The luminosity from her cousin burned her fingertips.

Brenda switched on the nightstand light, touched Angelique's face and braids and started crying.

Angelique held her, letting her cry for a few moments before pulling away gently. "What's going on here, Brenda? I had to go into the dream or nightmare or whatever that was to wake you."

Brenda sat back against the pillows. "They're after me, but now that you're here it's going to be all right."

"What was all that?"

"You were in the dream?" Brenda asked.

Angelique nodded.

"I thought I was imagining you," Brenda rubbed her forehead with her fingertips. "Did you see them?"

Angelique shook her head. "I'm not sure what I saw. It was jumbled. Voices and images I couldn't make out. They said your name backwards with such power."

Brenda ran her fingers through her short-cropped curls. "I wanted to call you before now but I was afraid they would go after you. This attack came while I was asleep. If you hadn't come in, I don't know how much longer I could have held out." She took a gulp of water from a bottle at the nightstand. "Remember how we combined our power when we were kids and saved Grandmom from that ghost?"

Angelique rubbed the tension out of the back of her neck. "That didn't feel like a ghost. It felt like a living person with a lot of power. Does this involve the Order?"

Brenda nodded. "I think it's someone in the Order. You and Grandmom were right. Magic and groups of humans don't go together. Too much ego involved. I left them."

"What about Flynn?" Angelique asked.

Brenda closed her eyes. "We're over."

Angelique breathed through the intense, tingling light coming from her cousin. "I'm sorry. You two were so good together."

Brenda shook her head. "Well, it's better this way. He'll be safer without me."

She slumped back against the pillows. "While I was in the Order I met wonderful people. It was great being able to talk openly about magic with others. We had an influx of new members in the last six months and there was a subtle change in the group's dynamics, some underlying negative power.

"Flynn and I talked about it, and he brought it to the attention of the executive board of the Order. There was an investigation. They found no evidence of magic being used in a dark manner." She stopped and rubbed her forehead.

"Are you all right?" Angelique asked.

"No-no. It's hard talking about the Order, even to you. When I left I had to accept a silence spell to keep certain facts about the Order secret. We're so close the spell doesn't detect you as a separate person. It's as though I was talking to myself, but even with that it's hard." She took another drink of water and chanted in a whisper:

"My mind is one
I am alone
The binding holds
The binding holds."

"Maybe you shouldn't — " Angelique started to say.

"No, I'll be okay.

"So, the executive board didn't find anything wrong, but I was having strange dreams of being controlled and held. The more I slept the more tired I became. My work began to suffer. I couldn't concentrate. I decided to leave the Order. Flynn and I argued. It was terrible. He kept saying it was Gray Magic."

"Your magic turned negative back to you?" Angelique asked.

"Right, as if I haven't taken into account the repercussions of magic I've done. I may seem reckless, but not with magic. I'd know the difference anyway."

Brenda pulled her knees up and wrapped her arms around them.

"Anyway, the dreams became worse after I left the Order. I started losing the line between waking and sleeping. Even when I was awake I felt like someone else was looking through my eyes. I began making mistakes at work. My latest project was suffering, so I took time off. I'd hoped to find out more about who was involved, but they're hiding too well." She shook her head. "I can feel them when I wake. Shadows, like birds flapping in my mind. They're very strong."

"Do you have any idea who it is?" Angelique asked.

Brenda closed her eyes and took a deep breath. "I suspect a couple of people. I've looked all over for some sign of something placed inside my apartment, some kind of charm used to link them to me, but I haven't found anything. Did you pick up anything when you came in?"

"Just your protective spell," Angelique said. "Although, when I woke just now, I thought I saw something move in the shadows."

Brenda grabbed Angelique's her hands. "What did you see?"

"Nothing I could describe. You know how we used to dream when we were younger and could shape the shadows. I don't think it was someone else. There wasn't anyone else in here except me and echoes of you."

"Are you sure you didn't feel anything else in the apartment?"

Angelique held Brenda's hands in hers. "Nothing else."

"What are they after?" Angelique asked.

Brenda looked away and then back at Angelique. "I don't want to say too much. It's better you don't know."

"Better how? They probably know I'm here since I had to break you out of that dream. You might as well tell me."

Brenda fingered a bracelet of charms on her right wrist. "It's about my work. I've been doing genetic research, working on gene therapy."

"What's that got to do with magic?" Angelique asked.

"I've been working on a personal project at the lab." Brenda struggled to her feet and stretched. She paced as she talked. "I've found something fantastic, Angelique. The thing I've been looking for."

"The magic gene?" Angelique asked.

"Something like that. Our team's been working with chromosome 19. Its network of genes controls repairing DNA damage caused by pollutions and radiation. You know how we've always wondered why some people have more power than others?"

Angelique nodded.

"I've found some sequencing data that implies chromosome 19 is making repairs in DNA that increases the ability for people to access their power. I've been doing my own research on the side, looking at my chromosomes and yours."

"Mine, but how — ?" Angelique frowned. "Oh, I guess you could have gotten a sample of my DNA from any of my visits. You should have told me."

"I'm sorry. I meant to tell you what I was doing, but I've always believed there was a scientific explanation for magic. I think nature tries to fix us and ends up making us different. The next question is whether we could manipulate someone's DNA to enhance or turn on their power. I'm afraid this is what they're interested in."

She stopped pacing and sat on the bed. "There was a break-in at the lab, but I don't keep the results there. I always downloaded the data when I leave. Two weeks ago there was a break-in here while I was at work. That's when I knew someone was after my research. Now they're trying to break into my mind and make me show them what I've discovered."

"I can't believe this." Angelique stood up. "You steal my DNA, do research I'm sure your lab didn't approve and now put us both in danger. I don't know how someone so smart can act so stupid sometimes."

Brenda shook her head. "You're right." She grabbed Angelique's hands. "But now that you're here, maybe together we can find out who's after me."

"And then what?" Angelique asked, pulling away. "There aren't any magic police to protect you. Do you at least have the information in a safe place?"

"Very safe. I'll figure a way out of this." Brenda looked at her watch. "Isn't Tempus Fugit playing at Sara's club tonight?"

"In about three hours, but — "

"I need to get out of here. Why don't you shower and dress here for tonight. We'll go to the club together. I'm starving. Sara's kitchen still makes the best po-boy sandwiches and onion rings around. By the way, how's Milez?"

"He's been fine."

"Good I'll give him a quick checkup tonight, free of charge."

"You still haven't told me how you're going to handle this — attack," Angelique said, leaning against the doorway with her arms crossed.

"Don't worry, I will." Brenda rushed to the living room.

Angelique closed her eyes and massaged her temple. She was going to need something for this headache and she had a feeling things were just going to get worse.

Angelique changed to the black body suit designed to communicate with Milez. Before they left for the Funky Piranha, Brenda stopped at the door. "Remember the protection spell you created when we were kids?"

Angelique nodded. They held hands and recited it together:

"Goddess of Day
Complete the way
Goddess of Night
Surround us with Light
I call upon thee

I call upon thee
To protect us two
Protect us twice."

Warmth encircled them. Brenda gave her cousin a hug. "I'm so glad you're here."

When they entered the club Brenda went straight to Milez. Angelique talked to Sara and the three members of her band, as she watched her cousin talk quietly to Milez with her hand over his open interface panel. Tendrils of blue protoplasm moved over her right hand and wrist, and danced around her bracelet.

She walked over to Brenda. "So what's going on?"

"Just catching up. I ran a quick check of his system and he's in excellent shape." Brenda caressed his casing with her other hand.

"I'm always good around you, Brenda," he said. Lines of neon light fanned out of the interface panel, filling the ceiling of the club as the protoplasm melted off her hand back into the container.

"Show off," Angelique said, smiling. "Save the pyros for the show tonight."

"Don't worry, I've got plenty where that came from," he said.

Brenda sat at a small table next to the long bar opposite the small stage. The sound check didn't take long. Once Sara opened the doors to the public, the small club filled up quickly.

Sara turned down the lights. The band opened with Combustion, an original piece written by Angelique. Milez made his way to the top of his casing in slow, graceful neon-bright blue drops, like rain falling up. Angelique rifted on the acoustic with one hand, the other hand lay over his open interface panel. As the blue protoplasm touched her hand it poured up and over her hand and arm until she was spotted with glowing dots. Milez picked up the sounds from the piano and broke the chords into sharp harmonic bursts to complement her playing. The bass, drums and violin danced in and around the main movement. The dots slithered and swirled into lines and patterns over her body. She played with her eyes closed, occasionally humming and scatting. Milez picked up her voice and morphed the sounds to play back against the original sounds. They teased back and forth, building and juxtaposing each other's harmonies. At the climax of the piece, Milez threw a rainbow of laser light into the air, the thin lines flashing into flame shapes overhead. The audience erupted into whoops and applause.

The rest of the evening went quickly. They played two long sets with a short break in between to a standing-room-only crowd. The band finished well after midnight.

Brenda drank juice with her meal. In spite of being at the club all that time, her aura was brighter then when they first arrived.

Sara locked the door after the band, bartender, and bouncer left.

"How about we have some of my best scotch, to celebrate the Three Musketeers?" Sara asked, as they sat on the edge of the stage near Milez.

"The three of us?" Brenda asked, pointing to Sara and her cousin.

"No, silly," Sara said, laughing. "You, Angelique and Milez. I'll meet you in my office."

"You enjoy the scotch. I dig the juice in your club, Sara," Milez said, sending sparks into the dimly lit room.

"You can have as much electricity as you like," Sara said.

"Do you need me anymore tonight, baby?" Milez asked

"No, you can sleep," Angelique said.

"Nighty-night, girls," he said. The soft glow of his suspension liquid dimmed and went out as his protoplasm settled into the dark base.

Someone banged on the front gate of the club. Sara pulled the curtain aside and peeked out. "It's the bartender, he must have forgotten something. You two go on, I'll be there in a minute."

"We'll pour one for you, Sara," Brenda said as they walked to Sara's office in the back of the club. "The band sounded better than ever."

"Thanks. It's been a long night," Angelique said, sitting on the small couch. "What are you going to do about your problem? You can't hide from them forever."

"I know, but I don't think I'll have to." Brenda sat in a chair next to the couch.

The office door opened and Sara came in. Angelique started to speak but the look on Sara's face stopped her. A large man and a tall woman came in behind her. Only after they shut the door behind them did Angelique see the guns. She began to rise when the Asian woman gestured with her weapon to sit down.

"Brenda, good to see you again," the man said. He had strong Native American features and wore his long hair in two tight braids, wrapped in leather strips. Silver and stone charms hung from his multiple earrings. Power vibrated around him like the sound of fine glass being gently struck.

"Mac. It's been you all this time," Brenda said.

"I had a feeling you knew that," he said, walking over to them.

"You know these people?" Sara said.

"Unfortunately we used to belong to the same club."

"Gun club?" Sara said, sitting down at her desk.

"You're funny," Mac said. "Not many people can maintain their sense of humor with guns pointed at them."

"You should come to this club during Mardi Gras." Sara leaned back in her chair.

"Mind your manners and you might get to see Mardi Gras this year," the Asian woman said.

Sara opened her mouth, then crossed her arms over her chest and glared at them instead.

Mac leaned over Angelique and caressed her face. "So this is your cousin." He closed his eyes for a moment and took a slow breath. "The power runs deep in your family. Imagine the children you and I could make."

Brenda stood and pushed him away from Angelique. "Did you come here to look for a wife?"

He grabbed her arms and pulled her close. "You know what I came for," he whispered. "We've played around long enough. I can't wait to get the information from you – even with my skills you've kept me out."

"Why are you doing this?" Brenda asked.

He released her and laughed. "You can't seriously be asking that. The potential of your discovery is obvious. Everyone wants more of what they have, whether it's money, beauty or power."

"You're one of the strongest in the Order –"

"This has nothing to do with them." He leaned against the wall opposite her. "They're small-minded humans doing little tricks. I have bigger plans that need bigger power. You've found the path and now you'll share it with me." He spread his hands in front of him. "Why fight me on this? Your resistance can't keep me away forever. Why not work with me? I'm certainly a better match for you than that wimp, Flynn."

"What's he got to do with this?"

"Nothing now." Mac smiled. "He has no more power than most people, making them very easy to manipulate. Like your albino friend here–a simple glamour spell and she believed someone she knew was at the front entrance."

Brenda balled her hands into fists. "You influenced Flynn to break up with me?"

"Should you be saying this in front of her?" the woman asked Mac, gesturing to Sara.

"Don't worry about her," Mac said. He turned to Angelique. "But you're worried about her, aren't you?" He nodded to the Asian woman.

She pressed her gun against the side of Sara's head. Sara reached up to push the gun away and the woman released the safety, Sara threw her hands in the air and slowly lowered them to her lap.

Angelique jumped to her feet. "Don't hurt her."

"Don't–I'm fine," Sara said.

"Yes, I thought so." He shoved Angelique back on the couch. "The air is thick with the attraction between you two. The thing is, I don't want to hurt anyone. I just want the information your cousin has gathered and then I'll leave."

"What makes you think I have it here?" Brenda asked.

"Because if I were you I'd keep it nearby and we haven't found it anywhere else. We could search every inch of you, that might be fun, or we could go a more traditional route to convince you to cooperate. It's kind of low-tech on a magic level but can be persuasive." He nodded to the woman. She took a slim laser knife from her jacket pocket, clicked it on and swiped at Sara. Two of her long pale dread locks fell to the floor.

Angelique started to stand, but Brenda grabbed her hand and squeezed. A spike of electricity rushed between them.

"There's no reason to overreact," Brenda said.

"Then give me what I want," he said.

Brenda took a long breath and pushed out. The air in the room compressed.

"I was waiting for you to try something like this," he said. He waved his hands in the air, clenched his hands into fists and grunted. The pressure in the room disappeared.

Angelique squeezed Brenda's hand and took a breath at the same time she did, pushing out from her center. They worked together, their power joining and pushed the air toward Mac and his partner.

"Sara, run," Brenda said.

There was a loud boom overhead. Light bulbs exploded. Their ears popped as an invisible hand shoved them away from each other.

Brenda ran out the door, through the club and into the crowded street. She turned around and saw Sara but not Angelique. Sara stopped and looked back at the same time.

"Keep running!" Angelique's voice whispered in her ear. She still didn't see her cousin, but grabbed Sara's arm.

"We have to get further away," Brenda said.

"What about Angelique?"

"She's okay. Let's go." She pushed Sara in front of her. They shuffled through the packed streets. Sara ducked into an alley and Brenda followed her as they ran left and right through the alleys.

They climbed over a low fence, through a yard, and into the back door of a bar. The bar was an old neighborhood hang out, a safe haven for natives when the French Quarter was swamped with visitors. Sara grabbed Brenda's arm and lead her through the crowd to the bar.

"Hey, Sara, what's up?" the bartender yelled over the jukebox.

Brenda looked at her and shook her head.

"Just out for a little down time," Sara said.

The bartender poured two beers into frozen mugs and slapped them on the bar in front of Sara and Brenda.

"We have to go back and get Angelique," Sara said.

"She's safe for now," Brenda said. "He'll use her to get the information from me."

"You know that for a fact?"

Brenda nodded and looked across the bar at the wide mirror. A shudder went through her . . .

. . . she was back in the club, sitting in a chair. She tried to move, but ropes held her tight. A silence spell kept Brenda/Angelique from talking. Through Angelique's eyes the images were warped and stretched.

"Brenda, I know you can hear me," Mac said. "It's fortunate that you and your cousin are so close. It saved her life."

Mac passed the laser knife in front of their face. "I can start carving your cousin up, or you can give me what I want. And just so you know I'm serious."

He walked behind Brenda/Angelique, she heard the high-pitched sound of the laser coming on. They struggled in the chair and screamed at the jolt of pain in her right hand. The pain dulled to a throb. Mac showed her a fingertip.

"I sealed the wound so she won't bleed to death. Just the little finger, above the knuckle. Something that can be rebuilt, but I can do more, much more." He waved his hand in front of her face and the silence spell lifted briefly.

"No, please, don't hurt her anymore," Brenda said, using Angelique's voice. "I'll meet you at the corner of Canal and Basin. Bring Angelique."

"I sincerely hope you're not going to try anything. I'd hate for you to experience the death of your cousin," Mac said. He shoved Brenda out of her cousin's mind.

"What's wrong?" Sara asked. "Are you all right?"

"Come on," Brenda said, pulling Sara out of the bar.

As they walked to the meeting place, Brenda explained everything to Sara.

"I don't need magic to know that he's dangerous," Sara said. "Do you really think he'll just let us walk away after he gets the information from you?"

Brenda shook her head. "At the best he'll use his power to scramble our minds, which could probably turn a normal person into a vegetable. You know what the worst case is. Angelique and I could probably fight off some of his power together, but I don't think we could protect you too. In fact, you should go somewhere safe until this is over."

"No can do, not while Angelique's in danger. I've lived in New Orleans long enough to suspect there was something to magic, but I'm not sure I can believe all of this," Sara said as they walked down the street.

"I understand your skepticism," Brenda said. "If you won't leave then you have to do whatever I say, whether you believe or not."

Sara nodded.

Brenda looked up at the entrance to the St. Louis Cemetery #1.

"We'll meet them inside."

Sara hesitated. "Not that I'm afraid, but I don't think cemeteries and magic are a good mix."

"I'm hoping not." Brenda said a quick chant asking for the blessings of the dead before they entered.

They walked through the rows of stone houses. The full moon made the white stone crypts and concrete ground glow. Brenda went to a brick wall of arches, burial holes for the poorer community. A couple of the arches fronts had crumbled, leaving gaping openings. She laid her hand on the front of each small arch until she felt the vibration she needed.

"Someone in here died angry and betrayed."

"What are you doing?" Sara asked.

"Trying to get us out of the mess I got us into." She put her finger to her lips to quiet Sara.

She pulled a piece of red yarn out of a small bag in her pocket. Holding the yarn against the sealed burial hole, she said:

"With this knot I seal this spell
You will not rest, you will not tell
Knots of red, knots times three
Bringing chaos and forgetfulness
From the rage within to thee
So mote it be."

Each time Brenda tied a knot she said the spell until she had tied three knots in the yarn. She bowed to the crypt, said a chant of thanks to the bones within and put the yarn in her pocket.

"Let's go," Brenda said running back to the cemetery entrance. They stopped within the borders of the grounds. "When they get here, I'll take care of Mac. You keep your eye on the woman."

A blue car pulled up slowly to the entrance. Mac got out with Angelique and the Asian woman. Mac walked with his arm around Angelique's waist and one hand holding the laser knife against her side. Angelique held her wounded hand tucked under her arm. She stumbled at the edge of the sidewalk. The woman held a gun down at her side. They stopped outside the entrance.

"Are you all right?" Sara asked.

"Don't worry, she'll be fine," Mac said. "A cemetery. Fitting if you try to trick me."

"The information is in a memory rod in here." Brenda pointed into the cemetery.

"Then let's get it and finish this," the Asian woman said.

"This way," Brenda said, leading them back to the brick wall.

Sara tried to talk to Angelique, but the woman waved her ahead with the gun. They walked past the sealed burial arches to one that was open. The concrete entrance had collapsed inside the arch.

Brenda put her hand inside, pushing aside chunks of concrete. "How do I know you'll let us go?"

"I didn't think you'd argue with sharing a forgetfulness spell between the three of you." Mac smiled.

"Okay." Brenda glanced at Sara and Angelique quickly. Sara stood next to the woman with the gun. Mac lowered the knife toward the ground. Brenda grabbed a chunk of concrete from inside the arch and threw it at the woman's head, hitting her in the face. As she fell backwards the gun went off, the bullet grazing Brenda's arm. Sara jumped on the woman and slammed her head into the ground, until she passed out.

Angelique grabbed Mac's wrist with her good hand and swung with all her weight, turning him off balance. There was a crack as his wrist broke, making him scream and drop the knife. Brenda rushed in and kicked him in the back of his knee. He crumbled to the ground. Sara grabbed the knife, sat on his back and held it to his neck.

"Don't move, Mac, or I'll activate the blade, and you won't care if the wound is sealed," she said.

Brenda pulled the knotted yarn out of her pocket and dragged the Asian woman next to Mac. She sat between them on the ground and placed her left hand on the woman's forehead, grasped Angelique's hand with her right along with the yarn. Angelique knew immediately what Brenda intended and let the fingers of her injured right hand touch the back of Mac's head. Brenda said:

"With this knot I seal this spell
You will not rest, you will not tell
Knots of red, knots times three
Bringing chaos and forgetfulness
From the rage within to thee
So mote it be."

Electricity shot through the cousins into their captives. Mac's body stiffened, as did the woman's unconscious body. Brenda said it again. Mac moaned, "No." The third time Brenda said it Mac's body went limp. The cousins closed their eyes.

They were falling in a dark sky. Thunder and lightning cut through the air. Four bodies tumbled in a circle, hands tightly clasped as if fused together. The first word of Brenda's spell echoed in a strange voice around them like the sound of a car crash. The screech of metal became winged creatures, their long beaks and tails ended in razor sharp edges. On the second word, the creatures swooped at them, using their beaks and tails to cut and whip at the woman and Mac.

Mac tried to pull away, but the more power he gathered, the bigger the creatures grew. The woman screamed uncontrollably.

The voice continued reciting each word of the spell with building rage and poisonous anger. Thick blood splashed on the cousins as the creatures tore and ripped away at Mac and the woman. On the last word Brenda and Angelique released their hands and opened their eyes.

"You don't have to hold the knife on him anymore," Brenda said, took the knife from Sara and helped Angelique stand up. Brenda's upper arm stung and bled where the bullet had brushed it. She looked at her cousin's missing fingertip. "Let's get you to a doctor."

Angelique laughed weakly. "You need to have that arm looked at, too."

"So, we just walk out of here and leave them?" Sara asked.

"They won't bother us again. Their memory is in pieces, ripped to shreds," Brenda said.

"Where did you keep the information they were after?" Sara asked, putting her arm around Angelique's waist.

Brenda turned and smiled in the moonlight. She jangled the charm bracelet in the air. "Mac was right. I always carried the data with me, but tonight I downloaded it somewhere even safer."

"Tonight?" Angelique asked, leaning against Sara. "You put it in Milez."

Brenda smiled.

How to Recognize Your Friend Has Become a Demon

They won't cross the threshold to your home
without a spoken invitation, snarling when you
    ask if they will go to church with you.

You find strange patterns draw in chalk under
your bed after they have visited, your pets
    suddenly begin to disappear.

They ask for your first born as a birthday
gift, avoiding the mirrors in your house
    saying they're having a bad hair day.

You dream you ran away with them
to the Circus of Lost Souls, upon waking
    you see red circus tents on the horizon.

They begin to smell like sulfur,
giggling when you tell them
    someone has died in your family.

They take you to the crossroads
at midnight for a party, you offer
    your soul as a door prize.

Photo by Stu Jenks

About the Author

Linda Addison grew up in Philadelphia, the oldest of nine children and began weaving stories at an early age. She moved to New York after college and has published over 200 poems, stories and articles. Addison is the award-winning author of *Being Full of Light, Insubstantial* (Space & Time Books) and the first African-American to receive the HWA Bram Stoker Award. Catch her work in *Genesis: An Anthology of Black Science Fiction, Dark Faith* and *New Blood* anthologies.

She is founding member of a writers group, CITH (Circles in the Hair), since 1990 and a member of the Horror Writers Association (HWA), Science Fiction and Fantasy Writers of America (SFWA), Science-Fiction Poetry Association (SFPA).

See her site, http://www.lindaaddisonpoet.com, for the latest information.

Photo by Beth Gwinn

About the Artist

Jill Bauman has been a freelance illustrator/designer for 32 years. In that time she has produced hundreds of covers for horror, mystery, fantasy, science fiction, best-selling books and other products.

She has illustrated works by Stephen King, Harlan Ellison, Peter Straub, Lilian Jackson Braun, Charles L. Grant, Robert McCammon, Richard Laymon, Jack Williamson, Hugh B. Cave, Fritz Leiber, Michael Resnick, J. G. Ballard, Stuart O'Nan and Justin Cronin.

Jill has been nominated for the World Fantasy Award five times and nominated for the Chesley Award several times. Her art has been exhibited at the Delaware Art Museum, the Moore College of Art, Science Fiction Museum of Seattle, NY Art Students League and the NY Illustrators Society.

Jill lives in Queens, New York.

Other Books by Linda Addison

Animated Objects

A first collection of poetry and prose, some original, some reprinted from such sources as Asimov's Science Fiction Magazine and Pirate Writings Magazine. Includes an introduction by Barry N. Malzberg and "Little Red in the Hood," on the Honorable Mention list in the Tenth Annual Year's Best Fantasy & Horror (1997).

"Addison has enough invention for two writers. And enough heart for three."

— Terry Bisson

Space & Time Books:
ISBN 0-917053-09-5 (paper) $7.95
ISBN 0-917053-10-9 (hardcover) $14.95

Being Full of Light, Insubstantial

An exciting collection of 100 poems, most never seen before, from the first African-American to receive the Horror Writers Association's coveted Bram Stoker Award!
Original photography and variations by Brian J. Addison.

"... is poetic achievement as solid and well-founded as a palace cornerstone. And that palace rings with the thrum and cadence of voice, weaving tales and songs full of fantasy and myth that will sweep you down from the eaves and up to the towers."

— Tom Piccirilli, author of THE MIDNIGHT ROAD

Space & Time Books:
ISBN 978-0-917053-16-0 $10.00
Received Bram Stoker award

How to Recognize a Demon Has Become Your Friend

Consumed, Reduced to Beautiful Grey Ashes

A collection of poetry to capture the path between things gone bad and transformation.

"...reveals the little horrors of the days, the curiously individual science fictions of the nights, the fantasies where 'tomorrow will be reborn'."

— Charlee Jacob

Space & Time Books:
ISBN 0-917053-13-3 $7.00
Received Bram Stoker award

Made in the USA
Coppell, TX
09 December 2022

88310443R10069